THE ADVENTURES OF SILAS FREETHORN:
A Puritan Tale

D.J. RENNER

THE ADVENTURES OF
SILAS FREETHORN:

A Puritan Tale

©2015 by D.J. Renner. All Rights Reserved.
2nd paperback edition, printed 2017

Illustration back cover ©2015 by S.A. Wood

ISBN: 978-0-9990196-1-0

Printed in the United States of America

Also by D.J. Renner
Raising Dad, Using Middle School Rules

Available at djrennerbooks.com or amazon.com
For School, bulk orders or author appearance information, please e-mail
darrinrenner@gmail.com for further information and pricing.

THE ADVENTURES OF SILAS FREETHORN:

A Puritan Tale

Leah,
There is an
adventure in all
of us!

Dedication

I dedicate this book to my family,
thanks for always supporting
my dreams.

Author's Note

Throughout this book there are many words used that relate to history. Some of these words are in *italics*. In the back of this book, there is a glossary called **Words of Historical Significance**. The definitions of the words in *italics* are provided in this section.

Silas' story is divided into four sections. Each section or BOOK begins with historical background information to help the reader to better understand the story as it unfolds.

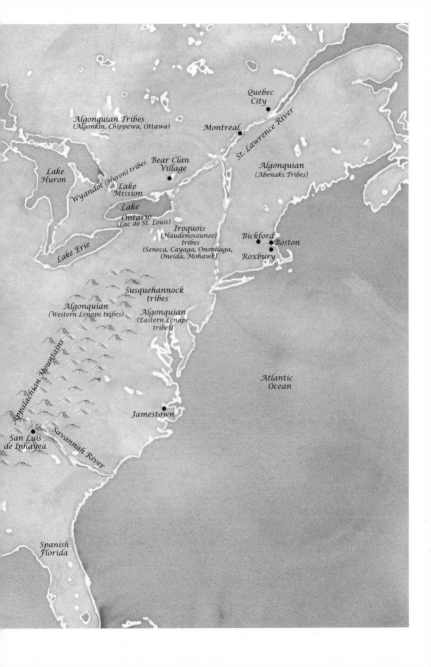

Contents

THE ADVENTURES OF SILAS FREETHORN:

A Puritan Tale

D.J. RENNER

Foreword

Spring, 1641

The crowd was angry, outraged, many were screaming and as I looked at their faces many were twisted in fury. I was seven years old. Mr. Ames, whose demeanor was always calm and gentle at church, was yelling and spitting with a look of rage. Others in the crowd were behaving in a similar way. Numerous people held rotten vegetables or rocks. My father opened a bag and handed my brother and me an ear of corn already broken in half. A large portion was blackened so it would not be wasteful. "The sinner will appear soon," Father said with an air of assurance. The already raucous gathering now grew even more animated as a man was led toward the *meetinghouse* in the center of town. The crowd parted and two male church members pushed the man forward. People began to throw whatever objects they possessed at the man. I watched in horrified silence as object after object connected and the man grunted and grimaced in obvious pain. I noticed some children being held up by adults so they could have a clearer shot at the man. Mother and Father stood several steps behind us captivated by the disturbing scene that was unfolding. As the man approached, some other adults next to us in the crowd pushed my brother and me forward. Those nearby encouraged us to launch our projectiles at the defenseless man. I was astonished as my brother reached back and threw his pieces of corn as hard as he could. One piece hit the man on the side of his neck. My brother looked at me with anticipation and nodded his head in a show of support. Everything felt wrong to me. A tear came creeping out of my eye as I stood motionless with my hands down at my sides. Someone nearby screamed encouragement, "Throw it Silas!" My brother briefly wagged his head from one side to the other in a disappointed manner as he slowly removed the objects from my hands and savagely launched them at the man.

Fearful of having disappointed Father, I turned to survey his face for a reaction. If he had witnessed my actions, there was no evidence of it. The man was led to the wooden *stocks* where his head and hands were placed in between two pieces of wood with holes cut out to keep him trapped. His head and hands were still exposed to the crowd. Some of those gathered saved their objects for this moment and now threw them at the man. Most thumped harmlessly off the wood of the contraption but one caught the man on the side of his mouth. Blood and spit immediately burst from his mouth. A long string of drool hung from his lip for a long time. Small cuts were also visible on his face and hands. I found out later he would be there for a full day. This man was a thief. I left the gathering feeling like a failure but I couldn't understand why.

BOOK 1

The Puritans

The Puritans were a very religious group of people (like the better known Pilgrims) *that left England and headed to the New World hoping to gain the power to worship freely. They wanted to purify the Church of England by repairing changes that had occurred over the previous few decades. The Puritans were seeking new opportunities and better lives, however unlike most early English colonists to the New World, the Puritans were prepared for the harsh conditions. The first Puritan groups to brave the frigid Atlantic and migrate to the inviting shores of Massachusetts Bay traveled in large numbers on multiple ships. They planned well and came to North America with many necessary supplies. Most early English colonies prior to the Puritans, in the early 1600s, began with one ship, fewer than one hundred settlers, and few supplies. In contrast, whole towns of Puritans crossed the ocean and re-established themselves in the New World. In a little over a decade, beginning in 1630, over 15,000 Puritans had moved to the Massachusetts Bay colony. They focused on eliminating corruption, demanding a strong work ethic, stressing unity, and dealing strictly with sinful behavior and actions while establishing "a city upon a hill" (from the Old Testament of the Bible) to set an example of living for all others. Unlike other colonies that were dominated by young males seeking economic gains, the Puritans established colonies built around families and community. They established order, lived remarkably long lives for the time period, and had success in farming and developing trade. However, some historians would point out that despite many successes, the Puritan leaders were remarkably intolerant of those whose actions or behaviors threatened to harm the community's standing in the eyes of God. Those who questioned individuals who held power or threatened the community's good standing were often dealt with severely.*

The Puritan Way

Chapter 1

My name is Silas Freethorn and I have a tale to tell.
I was born in 1634. I was raised in Roxbury, Massachusetts. Roxbury is a Puritan town to the very
core. My parents, Abner and Rebecca Freethorn,
crossed the mighty Atlantic with my older brother
Micah as part of the early wave of settlers during
a great migration of religious reformers. My father
speaks of those days with great pride and is in-
sistent that my brother and I understand and
remember these stories. He insists that the success
of our towns is strongly linked to the sacrifice and
efforts of all community members. We are very
dedicated to the church, my father and brother
especially so. Every part of our lives is steeped in
religious practices and traditions. We work hard
and study hard to prove that we are deserving of
our place with the Lord. In our communities, children are educated so they can read and interpret

the Bible. We are raised to believe that those who are lazy or wasteful are dangerous to the prosperity of the whole community. Rebellious actions or words are not accepted nor tolerated and there are stories from many communities of people being exiled for questioning authority or behaving in a way that jeopardizes a community's standing with God. One such story is that of Anne Hutchinson, her story is known throughout our towns and is used as an example of how God punishes those on the wrong path. Hutchinson attracted a religious following of both men and women; she held meetings in her home in Boston. Her leadership challenged the accepted role for a woman and she was eventually charged by local magistrates for actions unbecoming of a woman. After a very controversial trial in which Hutchinson defended herself well, she was banished from the colony. She later suffered a horrific death at the hand of savages in Dutch New Amsterdam.

Church leaders remind us, through these stories, that those who don't repent suffer the wrath of God. Our rules and laws are very clear and threats to the success and peace in the community are dealt with harshly and quickly. Every community has individuals that have tested the rules and suffered the consequences, much like Anne Hutchinson. Criminal behavior, quarrelsome couples, *nightwalking*, disobedience, rebelliousness, and failing to conform to community norms could all lead a person to the stocks or whipping post. Each town had stocks or shackles where a person was restrained in the center of town as a means of public humiliation. When we were young, we were sometimes encouraged to throw rotten vegetables or stones at those serving time in the stocks. Church leaders frequently reminded us during services of the fate of the unfortunate souls who were repeatedly tempted by the Devil in some way. I felt at an early age I was different.

Chapter 2

My brother Micah's name roughly means "he who is like God." The name Silas means "man of the woods." In Puritan society, names and their meanings are very important. My mother always loved to tell us simple things like this. I remember thinking when I was young how my mother must be similar to what an angel in heaven is like. She could restore internal peace in me with a sympathetic glance or gentle touch after being "corrected" for some minor offense. "Ruling the child" was common and expected of male head of households in our community. My father was a stern, serious man. He had poured his heart and soul into his religion and his community and had no doubts that the path he had chosen was the right one for himself and his family. He was extremely hard-working and expected the same from everyone around him. He loved us with all his heart and soul. I had no doubt in this. I remember a conversation I overheard between my father and Reverend Washburn, our church leader, when I was eleven or twelve years old. Reverend Washburn greeted my father in front of our weathered barn. Father must have forgotten that I was finishing up cleaning Hope's stall. Hope was a chestnut Galloway pony that we depended on greatly to be successful with each year's plantings and harvests.

"It appears you've had another successful day Abner," Reverend Washburn began.

"The Lord has been smiling upon us for some time," Father responded.

"He has for some time indeed. The fields are flourishing and England's demand for our lumber has seen no decline. Our prosperity is justification of our unbending faith. You and the boys will be joining us for the *barn raising* at the newly settled Hobbs place I hope."

"As is our Godly duty Reverend, it brings us great joy to see new members joining our community."

"I have heard from Schoolmaster Wood that your eldest boy, Micah, continues to excel in his studies. It seems clear he is on the path the Lord has intended for him. I have no doubt he is destined to be a leader of men in both mind and spirit."

"We are very proud of the boy, Reverend Washburn," my father's hard shell seemed to soften as he responded.

"How goes it with your younger, Silas?" the Reverend prodded.

"He is spirited Reverend, but I have no doubt that the messages of the good book will begin to take shape for him soon," Father responded apologetically.

"He was seen again recently on the west end of Samuel Birdwell's fields by his wife, Faith, dawdling Tuesday last for a period of time." After a slight hesitation he continued, "Let us be reminded of Proverbs 10:4 Abner; He becometh poor that dealeth with a slack hand: but the hand of the diligent maketh rich. I trust you have been doing your part to rule that child Abner," Reverend Washburn cautioned.

"He is a good boy, still young… but good." Father responded and changed the subject by offering the reverend some wood and making arrangements to deliver it the following day.

I was shocked! I knew that the adults in our community were dedicated to instilling proper practices and behaviors to make the younger generation valuable community members. I now understood that they watched us and even spoke of our progress. I was most surprised that my father seemed ashamed and disappointed in me. It was clear this was not the first time he and Reverend Washburn had spoken about me. Both appeared to be concerned about the way I behaved because I enjoyed stealing away to the woods or fields sometimes to breathe and be by myself.

I sometimes felt pressure from our daily lives. My father and brother lived their lives so intent on being perfect in every moment. I never felt this way. I am sure my mother was more like me, although we never once talked about it. There were times when my mother appeared to exhale softly when my father or brother left the room. It was as if in their presence, she was trying to be something she was not. When we were alone, my mother was different. She was more talkative and tender…not afraid to show her emotions. I was never sure if something changed in me or in my father after that day. From that day forward I noticed a difference in how I was treated by him. He had less patience with me. I was "corrected" often and sometimes I was not even sure what I had done wrong. I began to wonder if it had always been this way and the conversation I had overheard just made everything clearer to me. The feeling that I was a disappointment to him began to grow and fester in my heart. I began to understand slowly, over time, the only way for me to please Father was to become something or someone I was not, like my mother had. It didn't matter how far into the woods I went or how good my excuse was to steal away, I always felt I was being doubted by my father and watched by the community. Roxbury had become my *purgatory*, and until I changed to be someone I was not, in purgatory I would stay.

I witnessed my first hanging at 12 years old. This was not the first public execution in the Massachusetts Bay colonies. Stories had been relayed to us in the meetinghouse by our reverend. We were cautioned that choosing a sinful path, in league with the Devil, would ultimately lead to our demise and an eternity of punishment. John Wills had chosen that path. He had served time in the stocks and been publicly whipped for sins he had committed in his youth and early adulthood. It seemed to me most of his recent trouble came from his refusal to take a wife. Seemingly disgusted members of the church community constantly discussed his choice of a solitary life in angry tones. He was condemned in a trial administered by the local *magistrate* who visited our town several times each year. A jury of twelve townspeople had determined his guilt. He was officially charged with being a traitor. The charge was the result of his unauthorized trade with local Indians that witnesses claimed resulted in the abduction of two local children. The magistrate's sentence spread through the village like wildfire. It seemed everyone was involved in planning and preparing for the hanging. It felt more like we were preparing for a celebration. It seemed the whole town had gathered at the edge of the last field on the road that led to the old cemetery. The persistent early fall wind swirled gray clouds around in the blue sky as a backdrop to the stacked stone fence that framed dozens of aging wooden crosses. Several skeletal old trees stood spread out within the cemetery yard. The large tree that stood just outside of the rickety old splintered cemetery gate was prepared with the noose. The event began with a speech by Reverend Washburn. He stumbled to the front of the gathering. He appeared exhausted and looked slightly gray and sickly. After a slight hesitation he began his speech deliberately.

"It is with a heavy heart that I address this godly and determined congregation today. I have been the last several days at the side of one of our own while he faced his darkest hours. His is a story that man, woman, and child can all prosper from morally. His misguided behavior began with disobedience toward his parents and *blasphemy* against both his religion and church. The same hands that tried to save him and shape him became his enemy as a result of the Devil's influence. Poor judgment became his companion as he disrespected his parents, displayed surly behavior, and disobeyed the laws that unify the rest of us as brothers. The government and religious authority of these settlements has heard the evidence and implemented God's will to maintain our sacred covenant. The recent abduction of Leah and Amos Foster, our children, from Goodman Foster's own fields by a band of Abenaki Indians has tested this community's resolve. John Wills was in league with these same heathens and has continuously claimed he engaged them only for the trade of trinkets. He makes this claim despite testimony from two of our congregation who saw these Indians with whiskey, which Mr. Wills has been accused of bartering for with them in the past. We shudder to consider what horrors have been inflicted on these babes since their disappearance. John Wills chose his path from an early age. Many of you have offered your hearts and poured out your souls in an attempt to keep him from a wretched fate. I have worked feverishly to save him from the hell fires that await him through a proper confession. As has been his position in life, he has refused this help and inflicted blasphemy on myself as an instrument of the Lord. Like many of you, I have wept for this tortured soul. Let his death be not in vain, may the whole of the community recognize the danger that accompanies sin and the inflictions that plague the unsuspecting innocent when one chooses that path."

Reverend Washburn then gestured for the prisoner to be brought forward. Wills was slowly guided to the front of the crowd. Formal procedures were continued and eventually John Wills was asked if he had anything to say. A deadly silent hush came over the crowd as if this were the moment that everyone in attendance had waited for. John Wills slowly raised his head, which had been down throughout the proceedings. His brow was furrowed and he had a look of fury in his eyes. He glanced slowly to the left side of the crowd and then rotated his head to the right side making eye contact with some individuals along the way. He did not speak a word. It was clear from his actions that he felt he had been wronged. He was hanged in dreary silence until his kicking and jerking subsided and a gasp came from the expectant crowd. Quietly the crowd turned and in an orderly fashion walked back to town in deep reflection over the events they had witnessed. I often thought about John Wills's silence and wondered if he had also felt different.

Chapter 3

Abigail Reed glided effortlessly up the aisle of the church with her head slightly bowed. She trailed her parents by two steps and was flanked by her two sisters. This is my first memory of her; she was thirteen years old. She was six months my elder. Over the months, my anticipation of her arrival at church began to grow. She made the hours of worship more bearable for me. For the next two years, I found myself stealing glances at Abigail every chance I got. I came to appreciate the ever-curious look in her deep brown eyes, the golden hue of her skin in the warm months, and the sharpness of her facial features. Over time, I memorized each of her expressions of emotion and truly believed I understood how she felt on our religious days by simply observing her from across the room. There were times when Abigail glanced in my direction. I was never bold enough to hold her gaze. There was a perfection in her that made me content to just observe. The first time she spoke to me was so startling that I stammered over words of response for what seemed an eternity. She barely seemed to notice and instantly put me at ease with a patient smile. I realized later that she had sought out and seized an opportunity. My parents and brother had stopped to talk to others in the congregation providing her with the chance to swoop in.

"Another beautiful day the Lord has granted us with, Silas," she said softly.

"...I...It certainly...certainly is...glorious," fumbling for words as she peered gently into my eyes.

"Will you be attending the husking bee tomorrow eve?" Abigail asked referring to the community gathering planned to husk the large quantity of corn our community had recently harvested. The gathering would also include stories, songs, toy making, and games when the work was complete. One of the rare occasions the adults in our community found it in their hearts to allow some fun.

"I believe we will be going," I responded shyly, still in shock that she knew my name. Despite my habit of observing her, I knew her family was of wealth and never believed she would address someone from a family of our common position. Another aspect of the world we lived in that filled me with frustration and anger. We had strict rules to manage every part of our lives.

"Perhaps we can share in some toy making for the children," she said confidently. There was sincerity in her eyes, but I couldn't help looking around to see if I was the victim of some type of prank. Before there was a chance to respond, she had silently drifted away. My parents and brother Micah were headed in my direction. Quickly surveying the area for signs of Abigail, I caught her glance briefly over her shoulder as she moved away. We locked eyes just long enough for me to know that her intent was genuine.

This was the beginning of our secret friendship. Abigail Reed had a talent for surprise meetings.

She materialized in various settings as if she were a spirit and disappeared just as supernaturally when any chance of discovery arose. It mattered not if we were at a public gathering or if I had stole away for a peaceful moment in one of my remote hiding places. I came to expect her appearance and company. In the beginning, our conversations were simple, but over time she became my most trusted friend. She put my soul at ease and eventually I had a comfort in her presence that allowed me to share with her my most private thoughts.

Mother had sent me to the Harwood's place to drop off a crate of candles from her recent labors. This was in exchange for the butter Goodwife Harwood would churn. This type of exchange was common in our community. I drifted through the Harwood's corn. The early summer growth was just over waist high. My fingers brushed along the top of the stalks as I paused long enough to close my eyes and feel the gentle breeze blowing in my face and hear the rustling of leaves in the trees.

The forest, freedom, lay just ahead. There were precious few moments of time away from the pressure to act perfect and be perfect. Just a five minute walk from the cornfield stood two oaks I had discovered that seemed to embrace, creating a raised perch as comfortable as any sailor's hammock. I ran forward knowing that I would be missed if my absence went on too long. I set the crate at the edge of the field and burst through the trees letting the coolness engulf me. I took a deep breath and walked silently toward the intertwined oaks. As I approached, two feet dangled from the raised area in the trees.

"What took you so long?" Abigail teased. "One would think I have no chores to complete the way you plod along."

"Would you like to join me for a walk, Miss?" I offered with a hand extended to help her down from the perch. Abigail grabbed my hand and hopped down. I caught her just above the hips and returned her softly to the forest floor. Abigail gave a shy smile with slightly flushed cheeks as she skipped two steps ahead and proceeded further into the forest. After catching up, we walked carefully onward like many times before wondering what treasures and memories the woods would provide. We walked along, talking, joking, and experiencing the world together away from rules and traditions. Every time our arms or shoulders brushed together my heart beat faster and my desire to express how I felt grew. My fear of losing these moments held me in check. Abigail froze next to me as she extended her arm slowly pointing. She leaned in close and her cheek rested against mine. A short distance ahead in the forest was a doe and her two young fawns basking in a sunlit, grassy clearing. Ears and tails flickered as they bent forward grazing and once in a while, cautiously, each surveyed their surroundings. I could smell Abigail's skin and feel the warmth of her cheek. Her curls scratched softly against my face and our bodies supported one another. I stayed as still as possible. I was afraid to let this moment end. The deer caught a scent, probably ours, and quickly bounded away.

Abigail backed slowly away. "The time has gotten away," she said cheerily as she turned and bounded away just as quickly as the doe and her fawns had moments earlier.

Constantly trying to free up time in hopes that Abigail would appear, hurt my relationship with my father. Every time I was sent to pick something up in town or went to a neighbor's to drop something off or ask a favor I would steal away. When my father questioned me I had no choice but to lie. I could not risk losing my time with Abigail and had no idea how my father would react if he knew about her. He knew I was not truthful with him. His frustration continued to grow and I was growing too old for him to correct me with a wooden *switch*. There were times my brother Micah clumsily followed me. I assumed my father sent him to watch and report on my actions. On those days, I simply completed my task and returned home promptly. I sometimes considered telling my mother about Abigail. Without a doubt, she would eventually tell my father. It was her duty and responsibility as a wife to do so. She was a good wife to my father. I never realized then how big of a problem I was becoming.

My brother and I attended school whenever possible in a small, cramped one room school house in town. Schoolmaster Wood was strict but he appeared to love to teach us. Like the rest of our world his was filled with rules also. Education was designed to teach us the three r's, reading-riting-rithmetic while shaping our morals and values through religious messages in most lessons. Community leaders frequently stopped in to watch parts of the lessons. Schoolmaster Wood seemed very nervous on these occasions. My classmates acted mostly like miniature adults. Constantly reminding each other of the rules and clarifying whose position in society was higher. Abigail and her sisters were educated at home by their mother. I didn't try to make friends. Micah spent outside time with Abel Milton and Jacob Guthrie. This became my group as well. Most of the time we spent together I listened to them talk. They alternated between playing games and having conversations about girls and our community. They rarely found fault with anything in our lives. I never mentioned Abigail. Most of the time I spoke it was to ask questions to clarify their views on parts of our life. Why are there some girls we can't marry? Why is it a sin to hurt others but not a sin to rule the child and whip sinners? Why does God speak to Reverend Washburn as he claims but never to us? How can a thought be a sin if you don't act on the thought? They mostly seemed annoyed by my questions.

My anger toward father and the prying members of our community was growing in me like an intense flame. I had nearly reached my sixteenth year and was expected to be a man in my work responsibilities and community obligations, but I had to mask my emotions and hide my feelings like a scared child. The many questions I shared and discussed with Abigail about my frustration with our community began to turn to criticism and hatred. Abigail, my trusted confidant, had never hesitated to engage in discussions about our families, religion, community values, and anything else that I dreamed up. She had an even approach to such topics but seemed to admire and embrace any question I put forth. She was brilliant at seeing all of the perspectives in every situation. She would often insist that I recognize how my father, or anyone else we were discussing, saw the situation. It was extraordinary how she could see events in a completely unbiased way. Her approach rarely solved a problem, but it always left me thinking more deeply about the problem or issue. She simply brought brightness to any gloom and made me appreciate the moment we were in, rather than obsessing about issues or problems that were beyond my control.

There was a stagnant pond hidden by a thick patch of blackberry bushes just outside of town. Through the thicket, there was a gap that could be accessed by sliding between two old oak trees. This became our favorite meeting place. Abigail's father was a lumber trade merchant and had both a building and home in town. Over time, I realized this was the place where she magically material-ized most often. There was a soft scratch of twigs behind me as I skipped a stone across the murky pond water. It was a crisp spring day so the in-sects were not very bothersome. Abigail shuffled into the clearing with her hands clasped in front of her. Her brown curly hair framed her beautiful face as she batted her eyes jokingly, pretending to be flirting. She smiled as she began...

"You certainly are dashing today, Mr. Free-thorn," she teased.

"If only I could focus on the things of this world that bring me happiness...perhaps then I could be dashing like the heroes of our books," I responded thoughtfully.

"I cannot help but declare, Silas, that the older you grow the more glum you become. What trou-bles you so much that your eternal happiness is in doubt today? Yours is a good family in good standing in the community, your mother is kind, only your father is like a thorn in your side. I say, mend it, Silas. You have told me yourself many times that you struggle to find common ground. Use some of the wit and charm you use with me to improve relations with your father."

"I admit that Father is the central problem," I hesitated before continuing, "but it is the whole community, the rules, the way people condemn others, the unequal treatment, all while they march around with noses in the air like they are better people than everyone else. Even as children we have watched whippings and been encouraged to throw objects at criminals detained for public humiliation. Do you not see that we are a band of hypocrites? We claim to be a righteous and chosen people but our leaders act as if they are God himself. We are all prisoners! I cannot be me or be honest about my inner feelings in this community out of fear...it makes me sick," I spat for effect.

Abigail did not respond for a long time. She looked down and appeared to be considering her next words carefully. Through all of our years of meetings and friendship, I had never spoken this frankly about my anger and dislike of our community. We often discussed our families and events that had occurred, we even hinted occasionally about feelings for one another, but nothing nearly as bold and blasphemous as what I had just said. When she finally looked up there was a look of deep concern in her eyes. She finally began to speak:

"I need you to try...try and fix things with your father. If you're too stubborn to give in, well then, do it for me. The words you spoke just now are dangerous words, and I know that you understand the consequences others have faced for the same. I beg you to soften your stance and see the good around you and the possibilities that exist with time and patience." With that she spun and headed back toward the brush without waiting for a response.

Just before she entered the gap between the thorny bushes she hesitated and said coyly, "I have plans for you yet, Silas Freethorn," as if she sensed the sinking feeling in my stomach her sudden departure had given me.

Chapter 4

Three days after my meeting with Abigail at the dead pond, Roxbury, Massachusetts was re-introduced to smallpox. Once symptoms were detected, rumors swirled about victims first developing a high fever and body aches. The inflicted complained of head pain and a severe backache. Some claimed victims would moan and babble uncontrollably. As if the Devil himself, stood over their bed tormenting them. After the initial pains, the sick would develop a rash on the tongue and in their mouth. When the sores broke open and were swallowed, their fever spiked so high, the victim would sweat and whimper as if being cooked from within by hellfire. The rash spread over the whole body in less than a day. Some died over the next week as the disease appeared to roast their skin. If the rash began to scab, most survived. Word spread quickly after the first child died.

We all knew the danger of disease. Many blamed the Indians for sickness. They claimed the Indians' lack of religion brought God's wrath upon them frequently. Our community suffered for months. Dozens became ill and ten died.

My family was spared and we worked our fields like never before. Father was determined that we prove to the Lord our worth. My brother and I followed his lead and worked from sun up until sun down with a dedication that I had previously resisted. We were not allowed to leave our homes except for worship. Those who showed any symptoms of the disease were forced to stay home from meetings. Reverend Washburn gave spirited sermons during these weeks about the effects a sinful congregation would have on a community. He seemed determined to find a cause of the outbreak. Rumors spread about the families that had been inflicted. What had they done or someone else done to bring the wrath of God down on the whole community? Most believed that a person could be guilty of supernatural murder if they consorted with the devil or demons. Even the act of committing sins was seen by some as inviting the devil into our lives. After the first week, Abigail's family was absent from church gatherings. With each passing week fear and an ache deep in my stomach grew. I found myself praying to God each evening for her family's health. Word of Abigail's younger sister's passing brought me extreme fear and great sadness. I continued to work hard at chores but became even more disconnected from my family and others. Just as the rumors of sickness began to disappear the church and community leaders came for me.

Micah and I were chopping wood as Reverend Washburn and two officials entered the yard. Accompanying Washburn was Goodman Thatcher and Reverend Owen, who sometimes filled in at the church. Thatcher was responsible for detaining criminals in a room that had been built as an attachment to his home. Our community had no real jailhouse although one was planned. Reverend Washburn glanced in our direction with a look of disappointment in his eyes. He continued toward the house where mother greeted him before he had even knocked. Mother looked concerned but had a smile on her face and greeted the group of men cheerfully. Father was now headed toward the house from the barn. He also glanced toward me with a look similar to that of the reverend only seconds earlier. All of the adults headed inside. Although they were only gone a quarter of an hour it seemed like an eternity. My first thoughts were that something had happened to Abigail. But as I reasoned through the situation, I reminded myself that no one knew about us so that couldn't be the reason they had come. Perhaps they were just checking the health of each family. When mother began to cry I knew something was dreadfully wrong. My father and the other men emerged from our home trailed by my mother who was whimpering as she tried to hold back sobs. The men stopped as my father continued to advance toward Micah and me. My father walked up to me with slumped shoulders and a defeated look on his face.

"Silas, you must go with these men now. You have been accused of blasphemy and murder and will stand trial upon the next arrival of this territory's magistrate. There are witnesses who have come forth and reported you out of concern for the masses. One of us will bring your personals once you are settled in a holding cell at Goodman Thatcher's home. We will do our best to support you through your ordeal but you have brought shame on this family," Father said with absence of emotion.

I stood rigidly and did not say a word. It felt like having been dealt a physical blow. It was shocking the way he had spoken such devastating news to me, as if he had expected it all along. His tone had been even. There was no hope in his voice and as I walked away from him toward the men a feeling of guilt began to arise, engulfing me. I looked into mother's eyes as the men approached. It was clear from the stricken look on her face she was heartbroken. She didn't say anything coherent, just continued to gulp deep breaths to keep from sobbing. There was no look of disappointment. Hers was a face of deep concern and loss. She was the one person I would be able to count on to be by my side. My mind began to spin as the men led me toward town. Who were these witnesses that had accused me and how could they believe that I was a murderer? I was innocent of that part of the accusations against me. An image of John Wills, the man hanged years before, popped into my mind for reasons I didn't yet understand. Despite the shock and intense feelings of betrayal that were causing physical pain in my gut, I did not cry or speak as we walked toward town at a measured pace.

Chapter 5

It was two days later when my brother Micah brought some personal items including my other clothes. He entered the warm, darkened room slowly. There were only two small openings high up on the walls in the common area that all three holding rooms were attached to. These two openings were far too small for a person to fit through but had two boards each nailed across to discourage any thought of trying. Each holding cell had a door with an opening cut into the middle large enough to stick your head through. The room I was in was dark, stuffy, and uncomfortable. There was a wooden bench that ran the length of the room and a blanket for sleeping. My brother asked how I was and if I was being properly cared for. His questions sounded rehearsed and he seemed nervous. I asked why he was sent and why it hadn't been mother. He replied simply, "Father would not allow her to come." After some more rehearsed questions I dismissed him from the brief visit to ease his great discomfort. I was angry that he couldn't give me more support in my time of need but more disappointed that my mother had not been allowed to come. She was the only one who could bring me any comfort in this predicament. As I lay down and used the clothes my brother had just brought as a pillow, I made a curious discovery. A secret pocket had been sewn (mother was the only one I had ever seen sew) into my spare shirt and something hard was inside. Inside the pocket were a small piece of *flint rock* and a small but sharp piece of metal.

Reverend Washburn also came to see me the second day and every day after. He usually spent an hour or more speaking to me about religion, sin, community, and asking me about my views and beliefs. The first two meetings I answered everything he asked respectfully but offered nothing additional and asked no questions of my own. My goal was to present myself as simple and naïve. It was clear someone had betrayed me.

Nothing he had asked so far clarified who had spoken to him. There were only several people that I had ever spoken critically to about life in Roxbury. The list included my brother; my schoolmates, Abel Milton and Jacob Guthrie; and of course Abigail. Each time he left I thought carefully about what he had asked. The third meeting followed the same routine until he stood up to leave.

"Reverend Washburn," I proceeded cautiously as he stopped and turned back to me, "from the questions you have asked I gather someone has accused me of blasphemy. You have evidence that I have questioned the rules and laws of our colony. I have been forthright with you in my answers and by now you understand that there is some level of truth to this accusation. I will continue to answer your questions truthfully. However, there is something that troubles me greatly. Everyone that knows me, knows I am a gentle soul. Never have I raised a hand to harm a person in our community. Who would accuse me of murder?"

He regarded me carefully before he spoke. "Sometimes my dear boy, our actions start a series of events that spin out of control. A blackened heart can be a powerful device. It can easily become a vessel for both demons and the devil. Even a small sin can be a deadly sin and both the sinner and their conspirators can be punished as we have seen demonstrated in communities throughout history. May God have mercy on your soul and reward you for your honesty in the coming days," he turned away and walked toward the door. He stopped and called over his shoulder silently, "We have word the magistrate is in the town to our north and comes here in three days' time."

Being held in that cramped holding room day after day had given me plenty of time to think. After Reverend Washburn left, my mind rolled over all of his questions in the previous days. His last statement had also frightened me. It wasn't only his solemn message or hopelessness in his tone and actions. The words he spoke were beginning to create a picture in my head. Blackened heart, conspirators being punished in a deadly manner, these words began to add up. There was only one person I had shared all of my feelings with about my father and the community we lived in. Abigail was the only person who knew me well enough to paint me as a blackened heart. The vague comments and unanswered questions shared with the others I had suspected could not have led to such accusations. If Abigail told them everything from our secret conversations, they would surely punish me and the sentence would be a public whipping or worse. The more I thought; the more it all began to make sense. Our last conversation, the sickness sweeping over the community, Abigail's sister passing of the disease, all could have affected her. Could she have felt guilty and somehow blamed herself or even me for her sister's death? Our community leaders were looking for someone to blame. Had Abigail become frightened and offered me up? She may have even done it to save the rest of her family. I felt sick. There was a burning taste coming up my throat into the back of my mouth. My stomach ached as if I had been punched. Deep inside it was not anger that was consuming me, but heartbreak. Then I thought about how I had stayed close to home for weeks during the sickness. Abigail could not have spoken to me even if she had wanted to. My mind whirled creating theories of what had occurred in her world. I felt betrayed.

Standing in that holding room, staring at the scratched and stained wooden walls brought back all of my memories of whippings and people abused in the stocks or shackles. There was a look of humiliation in their eyes when their own neighbors treated them as outcasts. The screams and shrieks and jeers of the crowd as people were stripped to the waist and whipped publicly. The bloody, oozing welts that appeared as the leather contacted skin. I recalled the furious look in John Wills's eyes as he scanned the crowd in the moments before he was hanged. The silence that spoke of a man who felt he was a sacrifice for a crime he did not commit. *Condemned* more for the choices he made and failure to comply with the rules, than for any crime they had proved. Was I another John Wills? How did Reverend Washburn view me? Did it really matter how this whole situation worked out? My mind was beginning to construct a clear picture. There was a path that the condemned in our community always seemed to walk down and I was on that path. My future was determined and it would not end well. My family would be ashamed of me and Abigail would not be a part of my future even if I survived this ordeal.

The first two days of my confinement, I had to relieve myself in a bucket that was then taken away by Mr. Thatcher and disposed of. By the third day Mr. Thatcher offered to take me to his outhouse. He likely made this decision due to how cooperative I had been or because my nerves had wreaked such havoc on my stomach the smell of the waste bucket caused us both discomfort. Thatcher had a home in town. Shortly after the town had been settled, there had been an addition to his home with the holding cells. Trips to the out-house behind his home became part of my routine after the third day. My nerves and anger by this point had taken away my appetite and made me feel sickly. At dusk the fifth day, I complained to Mr. Thatcher again of stomach pains. I had put on all of my clothes in multiple layers and began to shiver uncontrollably. Thatcher was beginning to look concerned and asked if I needed anything. I asked to go to the outhouse. As we walked out the door, it was still light enough to see but the sun had already set beyond the western trees. In that same direction, was the gap between the two trees that led to the stagnant pond, where Abigail had often found me hiding out. The trees were no more than one hundred yards away. I walked slowly, Thatcher kept his distance as a result of all the recent sickness in town. Noticing the space between us, I ran. In a zigzag pattern, I ran as fast as I could toward the gap in the trees. There was no doubt in my mind he would chase me rather than shoot. After an initial shocked pause, he began pursuit and screamed for help. His screams gave me a good indication that there was some distance between the two of us. When I reached the trees I didn't slow down. I could envision the path through the thicket and barely slowed to navigate the thorny bushes. The shock of the scene as I burst out of the thicket will be forever etched in my mind. There she was. Abigail sat on a log with eyes red from crying. The look on her face was one of astonishment when I burst into the clearing. It only took me seven strides to cross the clearing before I dove headlong into the pond and swam for my life to the other side. In the last step before I hit the water, it seemed as if she smiled. Pulling myself from the murky water on the other side less than a minute later I turned to see Thatcher just now pulling himself free of the last thorn bushes into the clearing next to Abigail. It was nearly dark but she clearly mouthed three words at that moment, and I'm certain it looked like, "I love you."

BOOK 2

The Indians

The Native Americans of North America were very diverse tribes. Most historians believe that Asian nomads pursued animals across the Beringian Land Bridge during the last Ice Age. As massive glaciers began to melt, these bands were trapped on the North American continent. These groups wandered southward in search of food and supplies. Many settled in regions where food and resources were plentiful. They developed lifestyles that were dictated by the natural environment. The clothes they wore and shelters they built were the result of the natural resources available to them. Over time, they wandered to southern regions and some even reached the South American continent. Eventually they discovered how to grow crops and established permanent settlements. These tribes created their own languages and ways of life. They competed with other tribes for hunting grounds. Civilizations emerged that were primarily centered around gods related to the natural environment that surrounded them. Some tribes were very advanced and even developed dominant empires in the years before the arrival of European settlers.

To most European explorers these tribes appeared to be savages with little advanced technologies and a simple, peaceful culture. Contact with people from Europe had a devastating impact on these natives who existed for centuries with little threat from disease. The introduction of many new diseases and the European settlers' advanced weapons technology destroyed many tribes. Historians estimate that 9 out of 10 Native American Indians died within two centuries (mid 1700s) of contact with European explorers who eventually settled in the New World. At first, Native American Indians tried to establish peaceful relations with these new settlers, but eventually they fought back and tried to protect the lands the Creator had provided for their people. Most tribes believed in a variety of supernatural entities that impacted their cultural beliefs. Among these entities was usually a Creator who was responsible for providing the natural surroundings tribes depended on for their well-being. Generally, a tribe shared the land and items provided by nature because the Creator provided everything. Native American Indians traded and interacted with the Spanish,

French, and English settlers in the Eastern Woodlands of North America. Along the coast of the Atlantic Ocean and throughout the Appalachian Mountain region alliances were made and broken constantly throughout the 1600 and 1700s.

Many Native American Indian tribes occupied the Northeastern Region of North America. The Huron tribes lived on lands in the Great Lakes area that is part of Canada today. The Iroquois or Haudenosaunee tribes that include the Seneca, Cayuga, Onondaga, Oneida, and Mohawk lived in areas known today as New York and upper Pennsylvania. The Algonquian tribes were spread all along the Atlantic Coast and Appalachian Mountain Region. There were many regionally based tribes including the Abenaki, Mohegan, Pequot, Wampanoag, Mahican, Lenni Lenape, Chippewa, and Ottawa among many others. The Susquehannock occupied much of present day Pennsylvania. Most tribes throughout these areas spoke dialects of two language families: Algonquian or Iroquoian. The Iroquois tribes eventually unified and expanded stirring up conflict with the Huron, Susquehannock, and some independent Algonquian tribes.

The Indian Way

Chapter 6

I ran until darkness slowed me to a near crawl. I removed my extra layers of clothing and tied them around my neck, waist, and arms hoping they would dry and fend off pests. After the sun set, it was pitch black in the thick forest. Occasionally, I crossed a clearing and could see a short distance ahead. I had always considered myself brave, but there in the darkness fear gnawed away at my courage. I felt like an unwelcome intruder. The forest had a pulse. In the dark, each crackling step felt like a living being was under my feet. Insects buzzed and animals chattered continuously in this never-ending nightmare. Bloodcurdling shrieks erupted from close by and my face and then body ran ice cold under the skin. Branches attacked my arms and face forcing constant changes of course to navigate around impassable brush.

The last days of spring were transitioning to the early days of summer. The realization that I was lacking many supplies necessary for protection or survival began to raise doubt in me about the wisdom of my choice to flee. I drank water and rested for a few minutes whenever crossing a fast running stream. Having nothing in which to carry water proved a challenge but there were many streams. My destination was west. With every stop I listened carefully for sounds of pursuit. The many sounds around me made this difficult but childhood experience had taught me the unnatural noises to listen for that were made by man.

Slowly, that first night, the woods around me began to brighten. I could smell and feel the dampness of the forest all around me. Curiosity and perhaps a tinge of panic led to a search for high ground. The search yielded results moments later. A small clearing provided an open look at the surrounding hills and a rolling valley to the north. The sky above was changing to blue. I gathered several sticks and rested, waiting patiently for the appearance of the sun. The sun hesitantly peeked over several distant mountains. The feeling that this sunrise had somehow turned the pages to a new chapter of life rose from deep down inside of me. After a moment of reflection, I carefully arranged the sticks I had gathered to mark the direction of the rising sun and to mark the direction toward the west. I walked backwards into the woods away from the arrow and found a thicket of brush to hide in. Settling cautiously onto the forest floor, exhaustion overtook me. There was a deep weariness that was brought on by a pounding heart resulting from fear and continuous movement from dawn to dusk. I awoke sometime later sore and confused. Many dreamless hours of sleep left me temporarily befuddled. After coming to my senses, I stumbled toward the clearing in a panic to find the carefully arranged sticks. Despite the sun having set behind the trees, it was still just barely light. Locating the sticks and seeing the direction they pointed allowed for continuation of the journey west. My father had taught me some basic survival skills. Wandering in the woods often had allowed for the use of some of these skills. During childhood, father had showed my brother and me some of the plants we could eat and others that would make us sick. This was useful, but without certain items survival would be difficult. The flint rock and metal mother provided allowed me to make small fires. Fires I nervously put out after a brief period for fear of being discovered. A gun, a knife, and a container for water were items that would need to be acquired. Despite the risks and moral opposition, I accepted that stealing these items was the only option. There were many outlying farms and neighboring communities that needed to be avoided. Contact with anyone would make it easier for any pursuers to track me.

Stealing a gun and a knife proved to be much easier than expected. The morning after my second night in the woods I began to search for farms. Frontier farmers working in the fields were cautious but often had to set items down while working. Years of sneaking around in the woods proved to be beneficial. After only a short search, a clearing became visible through the brush ahead and an old farmer was visible toiling in his field. He was bent with age and paused frequently for a deep breath but wore a continuous grin as he went about his fieldwork. His knife was sheathed in his belt and his gun was never more than ten yards from his hand. I admired him. He seemed content with his place in life and it was hard to imagine doing anything that would change that. I faded slowly back into the forest and continued the search. A short time later another field emerged. Creeping into the new clearing, a knife and flint-lock rifle with a leather ammunition pouch sat not twenty yards away on a large rock. There was no one in sight. Stealing the rifle left me overwhelmed with feelings of guilt. Without the gun the farmer and his family's ability to eat and be safe was compromised. Trying to replace the weapon would be costly and likely difficult for the farmer. The acceptance that I could not survive without the gun helped to ease my guilt.

Repeated failure led to desperation to gain possession of either a leather or wooden *costrel* for carrying water. The problem was the farmers carried these on their belts and rarely if ever set them down. After two days of spying on numerous farmers, it became obvious my only chance to obtain a leather container would be at night. Entering a home or village shop would be the only way to do it. Just before daybreak of my third night traveling in the woods, I encountered several fields very close together. After further exploration, a clearing with four houses spread about presented itself. A dog barked lazily somewhere far to the left of the clearing. I retreated back into the forest and carefully located a hiding place for all of my newly acquired possessions. This proved to be a very wise decision. Back in the clearing, I chose to approach the house furthest from where the dog had been barking earlier. The door was made of tree bark. It was heavy. I grasped the handle that appeared to be made of deer antler and lifted the full weight of the door while pushing inward. The door was placed back down carefully with only the slightest scraping sound on the earthen floor. Moonlight shone through the now open door to provide some visibility in the darkened cabin. Soft breathing of the sleeping occupants was the only audible sound. The smell of an earlier dinner still wafted in the cabin air. Hanging to my right was a costrel. Slowly, nervously, I extended a shaking hand toward the leather container. I removed the full container and shifted to retreat but not before noticing a basket on the table. The basket was full and the contents were wrapped in a cloth. A hunger pain made its presence known. My stomach constantly ached due to lack of food after a diet of only berries and roots for days. My mouth watered for a taste of the baked bread in the basket on the table five strides away. After just two steps, a nervous voice from the shadows to my left cautioned me not to turn around.

"Mister, I'm not aiming to shoot you. But a man will do what he must to protect his loved ones," the man cautioned. "Put your hands in the air and head right back out that door."

The rest of the small cabin's occupants began shuffling out of their sleeping places to get a look at the cause of the excitement. Thoughts of running entered my mind as I stepped back into the chilled night air, but facing me was another rifle-wielding farmer and the dog that had been barking earlier. I came to regret that the first man from inside the cabin, Amos Perkins, was not the person who decided my fate. Within minutes the occupants of the four houses had gathered and four men were engaged in a deep conversation about how the situation should be properly handled. Amos Perkins appeared to be a kind soul. He quickly emerged as my defender in the ensuing discussion. Two other men, one they called Owen and another named John were angry and seeking a swift and firm conclusion to the affair. The fourth man, I never heard his name, was quiet and seemed content to let the others determine what should be done. At first their voices were too low to hear, but eventually they became more animated.

"The way I see it then is with two choices, we either take him to Bickford and let them deal with him proper or we deal with it here 'n be done with it," the one called Owen offered.

"Up Bickford, they'll give him twenty-five public lashes for sure or maybe a short stay in the stocks before they send him on his way. We could do the lashes right here and save the days' lost labor. We are fast running out of days until harvest," John added as he looked toward Amos.

Amos was slow to respond. Finally, he spoke firmly but in a calm manner. "He's only a young man. He snuck in here with no weapons and only tried to take a drink and some food. Most likely he has run off from somewhere and didn't think it through. We would have fed him if he had just asked; the problem is he was stealing. We should ask him why he tried to steal."

"If he steals, then he will lie as well," Owen snapped.

John was nodding approval to Owen's statement but still countered hesitantly with, "Could it hurt to hear the boy speak?"

My mind was racing. As the sky began to brighten to the east, constructing a story that would make sense was proving difficult. Nothing would come. All four men were now staring at me and two looked angry. A large group of women and children of all ages had gathered twenty yards behind the men. Some looked afraid but more stared at me curiously. For a brief moment, I caught sight of a young woman in the crowd. Abigail Reed's face briefly appeared before reality returned and the understanding it was not her. Amos stepped forward and appeared ready to ask questions. I decided to speak first and avoid an interrogation. In the past, a good twisting of the truth had worked best for me with my father rather than outright lies. So that was the strategy enacted. "My name is Silas. I ran away from the community I was raised in six days past. (Considering their time concerns this seemed like a better approach than admitting it had only been three days.) The decision to leave was made hastily and if you were to try to return me there I would run away again. For this reason, I will not tell you where my home is. I stopped here only to secure food and drink after a week of eating only berries and roots and drinking water from streams. I stole only to avoid the possibility of being forced to return home. Please do not ask me to discuss the private family matters that have brought me here. (I thought they might respect my being discreet on this subject.) I had no intention of causing harm or taking anything of consequence," I concluded.

The two groups in the clearing were staring at me. Any looks of fear had disappeared. Many faces now showed looks of understanding so it appeared the story had the desired effect. Rebellious, stubborn youth was tired of the switch. The group of men held a quiet conference. They spoke low so no words could be heard. They were joined by the two oldest boys from the other group. Amos and Owen seemed to be the most vocal. In the end, they decided to take care of the matter themselves.

A modified sentence of ten lashes to my bare back and send me on my way. The punishment would be enacted immediately. I was instructed to strip off my own shirt while Owen retrieved a leather flogger from his home. The wooden handled instrument had multiple leather knotted straps extending from the handle. They had no shackles or stocks so the punishment was inflicted as I raised my arms and leaned against the side of Amos Perkins' cabin. The families had all gathered around but there was a dreary silence. Unlike experiences in Roxbury, most of these people seemed to regret what was going to happen.

Owen asked if I was ready and I responded with a nod of confirmation. The first 3 or 4 lashes were bearable. They hurt, but the pain was quick to go away. After that, each lash left a stinging sensation that would not abate. There was an intense heat and my back felt like it was swelling as if from multiple bee stings. The whipping was over quickly. Determined to be brave and strong the struggle to stay on my feet became a challenge.

Images from childhood of people receiving twenty-five or more lashes came quickly to mind as a new respect for their plight emerged. Amos Perkins and his wife were there quickly to help me keep my balance. They guided me toward their cabin door and helped ease me down onto a wooden bench once inside. Goodwife Perkins heated water and placed a warm, wet cloth on my back. After some careful preparation, she also gently applied some slimy substance on my back that instantly soothed the burning sensation. Amos recommended that I get some sleep. After a moment's hesitation, the realization that ignoring my aching body and exhausted mind was impossible. We met eyes briefly and exchanged nods of agreement. He helped me to a corner of the cabin that had been prepared with cloth over a pile of leaves and instantly sleep engulfed my battered body.

When I awoke, Goodwife Perkins sent one of her children to the fields for Amos. A boy a little younger than me sat in the corner looking extremely nervous with a rifle resting uncomfortably on his lap. Goodwife Perkins checked my back while we waited and reapplied the same soothing substance she had hours earlier. The burning again subsided. She assured me the swelling and pain would diminish in a few days with continued reapplication. She provided a bucket full of warmed water and a small mirror. It was impossible to ignore the haggard look of my face and dark circles framing exhausted eyes. The image in the mirror had changed dramatically in such a short time. My light brown hair appeared darker and previously sharp facial features now appeared to sag slightly. The warm water on my face brought a feeling of instant relief. Cupped hands splashed water to the crown of my head repeatedly. After only a short time, Amos (whose home I had broke into hours earlier) came through the door cheerily. He shuffled around the room and grabbed a couple items from the table.

"You have slept away a good portion of the day young Silas," he said with a laugh as he walked toward the door to exit the cabin. "Follow me."

As I followed Amos, Goodwife Perkins and the boy from the corner each trailed me by a few steps out of the cabin. Once outside Amos turned. His face changed and he gave me the look an adult gives you before the beginning of a lecture. Amos had a kind face. He removed his leather cap to reveal a pale forehead in contrast to his tan cheeks and neck. His face was streaked with sweat from his day's labor. He squeezed his hat in both hands nervously as he began…

"Silas, I understand you have your reasons for the decisions you have made. I am pleading with you now to think about what has brought you here and consider if there is any way you can fix your troubles and return home. You look worn after your brief journey. The path you are on is a dangerous one full of peril and death," he cautioned and paused to let his previous words sink in before continuing. "You will find scattered settlements for another few days west of here before you come to Indian Country. The Indians have been fighting between themselves and some are even using guns now. To the south you may find settlements for a ways and even find many willing to help if you ask. Whatever you decide please take this and good luck in whatever path you choose." He extended a tied up piece of cloth in one hand and the same leather container I had taken briefly the night before in the other hand.

Amos Perkins gave me the items and then extended a hand to shake. Goodwife Perkins scrambled forward to provide a firm hug and well wishes. I thanked them both for their kindness and assured them consideration would be given to his words. While inspecting the cloth later, I found it to be stuffed with fresh bread and a good portion of dried meat. The leather costrel did not contain water. It was full of *cider*! They were two of the kindest people I had ever met. After leaving the clearing, I returned to the spot where the stolen possessions were hidden, secured them, and quickly continued west despite Amos Perkins' words of caution. Perhaps father was right when he constantly claimed that I was a stubborn child.

Chapter 7

Amos Perkins had provided some valuable information. Head west for three more days and then turn southward now seemed appropriate for a new plan. I hoped to stay just west of settlement while heading south and eventually arriving in the first English colonies of Virginia. The leaders of our community had often criticized Virginians for their rumored lack of focus on religion. With the new supplies Amos provided, it would be possible to avoid people for a while. Over the next several years, the fact that plans seldom worked out would become apparent.

Three days later life took a path I could have never imagined. Settlement had become so sparse that travel during the daylight was now possible. However, because the insects were so bad, I kept moving until the temperature dropped over night and slept through the morning. The third day after being beaten at the settlement, I awoke to a dull soreness still engulfing the welts on my scabbed back. I had determined a goal for the day of obtaining fresh meat. After carefully loading the flintlock rifle, I treaded slowly through the early morning forest. Dew glistened off many leaves in the bright morning sunlight. Just before camping the evening before, there had been a stream with numerous tracks left by game along the banks. I decided to follow the south flowing stream for signs of game. After walking less than a mile, suddenly, sounds burst from the forest to my left. Something was coming toward me and it was coming fast. I aimed my rifle toward the oncoming threat and glared into the sunbeam-streaked forest. What happened next took place very quickly. Bursting through the brush fifteen yards away were three Indians. A young male in front was bloodied and beaten. The two behind, flanked to each side of the apparent captive, were older and done up in full war paint. The two older ones, warriors, looked ferocious and angry as they each carried a tomahawk grasped in their hand at the ready. The young captive saw me first and the fear in his eyes quickly changed to something else...it seemed to change to a look of hope or maybe relief. The thought of fleeing leaped into my mind first but there was no time. The older Indian on the right spotted me next. Instinctively and luckily, I dropped my body slightly to steady the rifle just as an unseen tomahawk sailed by just inches above my ear. It came so close the brown hair on my head actually shifted and there was a brief buzzing sound in my ear as it rotated past. Shock over the near deadly blow caused me to freeze for a few long seconds before regaining focus. As the tomahawk thrower closed to within three steps of me, the rifle erupted in my hands. A hole tore open in the area of his stomach and blood began to trickle slowly from the wound. The warrior's legs collapsed first as he dropped briefly to his knees before he dropped face first to the forest floor. As he fell, our eyes locked and the look of anger and invincibility from seconds before was replaced by a look of disbelief. The young Indian had initially lunged to the left to avoid the fray. The second warrior stood with a look of confusion a few steps behind the first. Blood was now flowing from a wound on his shoulder. As he struggled to stay balanced, before I could even move, the young Indian captive lunged at him with the first warrior's tomahawk that had nearly brained me moments before in hand. The tomahawk split his forehead as it connected with a sickening thud. The young one tried to pry the embedded weapon from the dead man's skull but failed. Lightning fast, he moved forward and grabbed the second warrior's tomahawk from his now lifeless hand before he stopped abruptly. He was only three steps away reguarding me curiously. Looking down, he knelt near the head of the first warrior. He put his hand to the warrior's mouth and hesitated. Slowly, he lifted his head and we locked eyes again. Then he smiled.

He slid the tomahawk into his braided leather belt and held his hands up in the air in a gesture like surrender. He then approached me cautiously and patted my shoulder before helping me up. He was speaking Indian words that I could not understand but he seemed excited and friendly. He wore only a leather necklace with beads on his upper body. On his lower half, he wore a blackened leather *breechcloth* with a bear painted on the front. His hair and eyes were very dark brown and his skin was darkly tanned. He had some cuts on his arms and face and a swollen lower lip but clearly by his movements, moments earlier, was otherwise uninjured. He was a hand-some fellow. He then began to replay the scene using a form of sign language. He held up his hands as if holding a pretend gun and made a noise like he was firing. He then made a sign with his right hand to indicate something was tumbling down, followed by the same sign with his left hand. It was then I realized, in the forest with what I had always been told were savages, this young Indian was telling me a story I understood. Out of complete luck I had managed to shoot both of those warriors with one shot. The musket ball had passed right through the first warrior's stomach and hit the second Indian in the shoulder. I would later learn that Gooheepagho (Lone Wolf) a Wyandot Indian had been captured, while hunting, by a Mohawk war party. He had been traveling with them for many days and they were taking him back to their village where he would likely have been traded or kept as a slave. Lone Wolf would become a close friend and the Wyandot Indians my new family.

Chapter 8

It wasn't trust that motivated me to follow Lone Wolf that day; it was fear. As he waved for me to follow, I was too frightened after the incident to stay there alone. We traveled together to the northwest for nearly a week. It wasn't nearly the same as traveling alone. He knew the forest; it was his. He was aware of danger well before it appeared. This was a trick that took many months for me to learn. We ate well. He taught me new plants that could be eaten. He constructed traps and one night, in a very short amount of time, he crafted a bow and arrow. He showed me how animals could be tracked using the signs the forest provided. He was a patient teacher even though we had no common language at first. He simply showed what he wanted me to know as he said the Indian names for items and actions. Some of the Indian words that were repeated often were easy to learn. After hearing the English version of the same words,

Lone Wolf quickly began to build his English vocabulary. He always laughed and smiled when we learned new words together. He learned my name although it came out more like See-lus with a pause between syllables.

The fourth day we came to a fast moving stream. Lone Wolf searched the area along the stream for a short time before he discovered what appeared to be an overgrown trail. Excitedly, he bounded along the path and up a steep embankment searching for something. At the top, he stopped suddenly and turned around toward me wearing a large grin on his angular face. He waved for me to join him. Upon reaching the top, a quick glance to the left revealed the source of his excitement. Hidden in a thicket of bushes and small trees was a splendid wooden canoe. The canoe had been carved from the trunk of a tree. The craftsmanship was remarkable. We spent the next two days paddling and at times dragging that canoe between streams. We were able to move at an incredibly rapid pace although learning to paddle well enough to keep up with Lone Wolf was a challenge at first. We came upon an amazingly wide river. It was the largest river I had ever seen. We paddled across this river and the current was very strong. On the other side we again picked up a network of streams. After days of navigating streams, we hid the canoe a short distance off of a more worn path and finished our journey on foot. Traveling and learning with Lone Wolf brought the first feelings of happiness to me since before the sickness had descended upon my old village. The sickness that had brought on a series of events and betrayals that forced me to question every relationship I had cared about.

The day we arrived at Lone Wolf's village was terrifying. I smelled the smoke from the village before seeing it or hearing it. I began walking slowly, falling far back of Lone Wolf. He tried to offer assurance it was safe but the stories from my past had created fears and biases that could not be ignored. After some hesitation, the courage to go forward was inspired by trust developed in my new friend. Everything I had learned and been told about these people turned out to be wrong. The sounds of settlement filled the air as we slipped through the trees into a massive clearing. We walked across an open area as rows of large wooden structures came into view. There were fifteen buildings constructed of wooden poles, logs, and bark. Each building had smoke rising through openings in the roof. To the left was a river. The village was built on a bend in the river. The opening to the river was about thirty yards wide and the forest on either side of the opening was very thick as the river curved sharply away from the settlement on both sides. There were hundreds and hundreds of men, women, and children performing various tasks in the clearing (I learned later over 900 people lived in the village). Young children ran everywhere laughing and playing. Some were watching adults performing tasks.

A group of older men had assembled in the clearing prior to our coming as if they had been expecting us. A few of them seemed happy to see us (or at least Lone Wolf), while others had hardened or even angry looks on their faces. Lone Wolf was greeted with pats on the shoulder as he began to speak to the group of men. He spoke rapidly and eventually made some of the same signs he had made when he told me the story in the woods. The group of men followed every word and looked more and more impressed as the story went on. Some glanced at me occasionally and a few even gave what seemed to be nods of approval. When Lone Wolf finished, some of the men approached and patted me on the shoulder as the rest began to disperse. Two of the men from the circle led us toward one of the wooden longhouses.

Most of the people we encountered looked on curiously. Small children came forward to touch my skin and clothing. Some of the younger men were clearly agitated at my presence. We entered the building and walked to an area where several women and children of various ages were awaiting our arrival. The longhouse was smoky and smelly inside. It was clear from the compartments built off of a center aisle that many families lived in each longhouse. Lone Wolf repeated the whole story he had told moments before. After he finished the story, he continued to speak and gesture toward me. He placed his hand on my shoulder and spun me around. He gently lifted the shirt to reveal the healing welts on my back, welts I previously didn't know he was even aware of. One of the women had tears in her eyes as she smiled at me. From that moment on, Lone Wolf's parents, aunts, uncles, older brother, and two younger sisters treated me like part of their family. I was shown a place to sleep and store personals among them.

Over the next few months, I learned from this new family and other members of the community. I was taught to hunt (using a bow and arrow and harpoon), build shelters, make canoes and tools, and communicate using a dialect of the Iroquoian language. These people were efficient and hardworking but still found time to enjoy life every day. They were the happiest people I had ever known.

They were loving people quick to praise and build children up and rarely critical of actions. The pace of their life was relaxing and not once was my new family too busy to show me how to do something or lend a hand. It was easy to become a part of this world and I awoke each day eager to learn, to grow, to live.

There was a small group within the village that avoided contact with me. The suspicious and hostile looks made me uncomfortable. As time passed without incident, it became easy to accept that some tribe members had reservations about my presence. Despite the insecurity brought on by the rejection of a few, growing knowledge and numerous new skills caused me to slowly begin feeling like a man rather than a boy in my time with the Wyandot.

In the early fall, shortly after harvesting had begun, tragedy struck for the first time since I had joined them. Talof Harjo (Crazy Bear), the chief of the tribe, had authorized the beginning of trade expeditions to begin securing winter supplies from Wyandot trade partners. Some of these groups traveled as far as Quebec City or Montreal to trade with the French. Others were sent to carry goods to other tribes like the Erie, Algonkin, Chippewa, or Ottawa. Goods, mainly maize, beans, squash, tobacco, dried fish, and beaver pelts (many acquired through trade with French fur trappers who frequently stopped at the settlement), were loaded into canoes to be carried to the various destinations. The mood of the camp changed quickly on that cloudy fall morning. Everyone seemed to have a new destination and a task to perform. Some men had begun gathering thick tree branches, vines, and long grasses and piling them near a group of women. The women were using these to construct what looked to be portable beds. It was amazing to watch the efficiency with which they worked. Women were mixing together animal fat and various oils to create black, red, green, and violet paint which some of the men had begun to apply to their faces and bare upper bodies. Although I had begun to wear deerskin clothing like the other men, I preferred to wear a tunic (that covered my upper body) that most men wore only in the winter. Morning mist was still coming off the river in a few spots as four canoes suddenly came into sight. Men dropped what they were doing and scrambled toward the river shore. I scanned the crowd for Lone Wolf but couldn't see him with all the commotion. Each of the canoes moved slowly and rode very low in the water under extreme weight. Large sacks were stacked not in, but across the middle and front of each canoe. As the canoes came closer to shore, the items that appeared to be sacks could now be seen more clearly. They were bodies. Each canoe was weighted down with lifeless, pale, desecrated bodies. I moved closer, unsure of what to do, as a large hand grasped my upper arm. Un'kas (The Fox), Lone Wolf's father, told me to follow him. At the riverbank, we picked up one of the mutilated bodies and carried it to one of the portable beds I had seen the women building earlier. Some of the dead had been shot by guns, many of the heads had been bashed in and other bodies had arrows protruding from them. It was a grisly scene. Of the three trade groups that had been sent out, two had been completely wiped out. Only one group had successfully reached their destination. They had recovered the bodies of the other two groups when they failed to meet at a rendezvous point that had been predetermined. Some of the Iroquois were declaring war on the Wyandot and other tribes in the area over control of fur trading routes. This same conflict had caused me to meet Lone Wolf that day in the woods months earlier. The whole village mourned and feasted over the next three days. The surviving family members of each of the dead men gathered his possessions and carefully organized them on the portable platform with the body so the departed would have them during their trip to the spirit world. The bodies were then carried approximately one mile to another clearing with close to one hundred small house-like structures in it. Around each body, men constructed one of these small houses just large enough to encase the portable platform the body was on. By the end of the third day, this ritual had been performed for all bodies. I was not there to see the whole process. When we approached the burial ground the first day, an argument broke out between Lone Wolf and a couple of the men who never spoke to me. One of the young men's fathers had died on the trade expedition. He didn't want me there. He claimed that the Spirits might be insulted if a non-believer was at the burials. Some of the older men mediated the argument. Lone Wolf asked me to leave with apologies. For each of the next three days, I stayed in the village while groups went to speak their peace with the departed. The fourth day after the trade party came back, the whole village returned to normal activity as if nothing had ever happened. They weren't the only trade parties slaughtered that fall. The Wyandot were tough, resilient, loyal people and I admired them for these qualities.

Chapter 9

Time living with the Wyandot passed very quickly. Learning their survival skills and language filled each day with a sense of accomplishment and self-worth. This lifestyle suited me. An internal debate was beginning to rage. Becoming a part of the Wyandot was unexpected. Feelings of belonging were not imagined; yet something was off. There was a longing in me. A hollow place deep inside that no sense of accomplishment or happiness could eliminate.

Winter crept in very slowly. Several French fur trappers began to ascend on the village and instead of trading their furs and leaving; they stayed. A few of them even had wives in the village they had married previous winters. Most Wyandot welcomed French trappers without discrimination as they had with me. Others clearly avoided the French. They were treated with respect, shared all supplies, and participated in most activities. All of the previous hard work made winter a very relaxed season. A large surplus of food had been compiled. The Wyandot (or Huron as the French called them because their bristly hairstyle looked like that of a boar) spent much of the winter months planning for the next year and telling stories of their ancestors' past exploits. The Wyandot believed that the best way to honor the dead was to share stories of their lives with their descendants.

Lone Wolf and I often took long walks, using snowshoes when necessary. The rounded toe snowshoes allowed easy navigation in the deep northern snow. The snowshoes were constructed using a bent piece of wood with a single crossbar. The weave was usually made with rawhide strips but Lone Wolf had constructed the ones we used from pieces of vine. The walks were a welcome diversion to spending time in the increasingly smelly and smoke-filled longhouse. Lone Wolf and I discovered that despite growing up in completely contrasting cultures we had very similar views and values. We became very close, a trust and friendship similar to that I had only ever had with one other. On one bright winter morning, while exploring the vast expanse of uninhabited forests, Lone Wolf stopped suddenly. At first, it seemed he had sensed or smelled game or danger in the area. However, it quickly became clear that the look on his face was not one of concern. Instead he appeared to be gathering his thoughts. A few silent moments passed. All around us the sun produced flickering crystals reflecting off the melting snow. He began to speak slowly, in broken English surprisingly, with a serious tone. This was not a manner common to him. Lone Wolf and I often had serious conversations but he almost always spoke in his native tongue and in a quick and excited manner no matter the topic.

"It good for me you here. You have been thank...ed many time for sav...ing me in forest. You have help me more after that. You learn, you work, you happy here. You not happy in old village. You not tell me words about the hurt on your back or your heart. Me think you hurt deep down in here. (He held his hands to his chest.) Me think hard many time how you much happy here with our people. Before you here, me not much happy here all time. Me take many suns to travel far look...ing for some-thing to make me happy. Me learn by you to be happy in this village again. You learn me...many... no you help me see some-thing me not see. You save me two time now brother," he finished with a deep breath and seemed almost exhausted by the effort of making the words in English.

Lone Wolf, much like me, had a tendency to question practices and traditions. Both of us had apparently searched constantly for a missing part, a missing ingredient. Unable to accept our worlds the way they were, we believed that something better existed somewhere else. It seemed we had both grown up in my time with the Wyandot. It made me happy that my appreciation of the way his people lived had made him regain respect for his culture. The finality of having no choice to return to my own home rushed over me in that moment. Even if able, I knew the lack of freedom would be unacceptable after experiencing life with the Wyandot. Lone Wolf had truly become like a brother. The changes to us both caused by the events of the past months had been mutual and positive but the words to explain how were difficult to put together.

I responded to him using his Native American language. "I owe you as much as you owe me brother. We are becoming warriors and men together." I paused briefly to nod and place a hand on his shoulder in an effort to show him the words spoken were important to me. After a few moments I continued by asking another question that had been bothering me for some time. "Most people in the village have accepted me like I was born to the tribe. Why do some members of the tribe not accept me like the rest?"

Lone Wolf looked into my eyes and examined me carefully. He seemed to be trying to read the emotions I was feeling. When he responded he spoke in his own tongue. "Some believe the white men anger the spirits because they believe in another. The French trappers who stay with us in winter speak of their "God" as if he is different and better than all others. Some Wyandot are always looking for something to blame when trouble comes. Most in the tribe don't believe the spirits would be troubled by such talk."

Despite his assurances, it was impossible not to recognize the similar beliefs in the two worlds that I had now been part of. When trouble came there were always those who looked for someone to blame. Here, like it had been in Roxbury, the possibility would always exist for me to be that someone.

Chapter 10

A young buck stood on top of a knoll a long distance away. With the steady northern breeze it seemed like an impossible shot given my limitations with a bow. Despite the odds, the cedar bow in my hand began to seemingly raise itself. I gently brushed curved fingers along the feathers at the end of the ash arrow shaft before mounting the arrow and drawing back the rawhide bowstring. Without hesitation the arrow was released and zipped through the chilly air piercing the target with a perfect kill shot through the heart. After gutting the deer, I ceremoniously raised the heart in both hands to the sky for the spirits to see and took a large bite. There was a surge of energy as blood pumped through my veins, bringing a feeling of being indestructible. The carcass suddenly felt light. Lifting carefully, the lifeless body was positioned over broad shoulders that had widened during the preceding months. The trip through the forest over downed trees and narrow openings was challenging but a steady pace was maintained. Blood streaked my cheeks and arms. Gliding out of the perimeter trees, I entered the familiar clearing containing the village to proudly display the fresh kill for my Wyandot family. My knees buckled causing a stumble before becoming frozen in place. Straight ahead a group of my Indian sisters and brothers stood yelling and shrieking at a terrified young woman. It was Abigail, my Abigail. The group parted and Abigail turned and looked directly into my face. Her initial look of surprise now contorted into a look of terror. Her shoulders slumped in exhaustion and the look of sadness indicated defeat had been accepted. Her terror-filled expression did not change as she continued to stare at me. She suddenly dropped to her knees and sobbed one simple statement, "I'm too late." I awoke and sat up reaching to wipe my sweat covered face. The images had seemed so real that it became necessary to examine my damp fingers to confirm it was sweat and not blood that had been wiped away. Dreams of Abigail were rarely the same, but she visited me often in the sleeping hours.

After one of Lone Wolf and my walks, toward the end of winter, The Fox and Hadawa'ko (Shaking Snow) my new parents were waiting for our return. Shaking Snow, Lone Wolf's mother who had willingly accepted me as another son after my arrival months earlier, seemed to be encouraging The Fox to speak to me privately about something. We spoke using Indian words. The Fox, as with most of the Wyandot elders, did not waste many words. He usually went right to the heart of a matter.

"Do you have happiness in your time with us, Tseeyee?" I had been given this name after I had spent many days a few months earlier determined to make my own canoe after being shown the skill. The name meant roughly, maker of canoe.

"I am glad to be here…" I paused before continuing, "…time here has made me more whole, solid." I used hand signals as I spoke unable to recall the word for complete.

He nodded his agreement before continuing. The Fox, like most elders, had a weathered look to his brown skin. His eyes were forever squinting and it gave him a wise look as if he were always contemplating something. Despite his age he was still sturdy and strong. He continued, "Does your heart long for your family?"

"I long for them," I agreed and then tried to clarify "...that home has no place for me now. I know now they are on a different path...a path I don't wish to follow."

"It is good when a man knows his path." He paused for a while to collect his thoughts before he continued. "A great honor has been put on you...a clan member has offered daughters for you to take as a wife. It is good in my eyes and early in my eyes...Hadawa'ko thinks it is not early for a wife." The conversation was not a surprise entirely. Lone Wolf had taken to teasing about a few village girls that seemed to be paying me special attention. Some gifts had also been left at my sleeping place recently. Regrettably, Lone Wolf was not here to give instructions on the proper way to handle this conversation. The last thing I wanted to do was insult a male member of the clan.

"It is soon, my heart longs for one left behind," I explained. Many times over the past six months in dreams, Abigail Reed was by my side through this experience with the Wyandot. In dreams, conflict raged over whether she was impressed or repulsed by the fact that I had become Tseeyee of the Wyandot. The evening by the pond came back to me. The words she had appeared to mouth as I glanced back across the pond in the fading light the night of my escape from Roxbury.

The Fox was patiently staring at me. I had drifted off into deep thought and he had recognized the temporary mental flight. When he was sure my mind was back he responded, "If your heart change, you tell me." He nodded and walked away seemingly content with the explanation.

That conversation brought many changes for me. As spring approached, most of the previous three seasons had been spent with the tribe. The thought of the future started to become a focus of my everyday thoughts. Even in the midst of a man's greatest moments and successes, the devil can plant the seeds of doubt. Or is it just convenient to blame the devil for our own shortcomings and weakness? Was this life supposed to be my destiny? Would the few overrule the many and eventually drive me away?

Signs of springtime began to emerge on our daily walks. Plans for a huge festival had been discussed all winter. Every tenth spring, the Wyandot Bear Clan held a feast for the dead. Days of events had been planned including feasts, ceremonies, and athletic contests. It seemed like an exciting time. The comments made by some about it having been only eight years since the last festival should have raised questions in me but didn't. Understanding and accepting the first part of the festival was difficult at first. The way it had been explained seemed savage and I had too much respect for my new family and friends to believe it would happen that way. It was shocking. The day the festival started the whole village walked to the clearing where the dead of the last ten years had been left. Each family opened the small structures containing the decomposing bodies or bones of their loved ones and removed the remains. We carried these bodies back to the village. Each family then scraped and some even boiled the bones before wrapping the cleaned bones in cloth. A ceremony was held each night where cloth wrapped sets of bones were presented by the descendants. The family then told a favorite story about the deceased that the whole clan listened to intently. The days were filled with feasts and athletic contests. One game they played was lacrosse and another involved a hoop hung from a tree branch. Tribe members competed by throwing spears through the hoop to determine the most consistent and accurate. Teams and individuals competed to gain status within the clan. The morning after the last ceremony, the wrapped bones were all returned to the structures in the clearing. Any Puritan who saw this festival would think these people were savages. Would it have been any different if Native American peoples watched a hanging? The English and these people would never see eye to eye because their cultures were too different.

One week later the tribal leaders announced plans to move. After early harvest in a few months, the tribe would move north and settle near Quebec City closer to their French allies and trade partners. Tribal leaders feared their Iroquois enemies would continue to disrupt trade and eventually attack the village. Groups would be sent throughout the summer to find a place for a new settlement and prepare the location. My first feelings were anger. This place, these people had become home. The perfection of this life would be destroyed. After a few days dealing with considerable frustration, a strange twist was entered into the troubling situation. The Frenchmen, who wintered with the tribe, were rumored to be heading southwest soon. A difficult decision would need to be made quickly. Was it my destiny to head north and make a life with the Wyandot in a new faraway land? Was my true path to the south following my original plan to locate and settle in the Virginia colony? I chose to go south.

Doubt can be a powerful emotion. Fear of possible rejection, becoming a scapegoat for some imagined offense drove me away. After becoming convinced that reliving the events that had occurred in Roxbury was a possibility, I chose to leave behind people I had come to care deeply about. Never before had I been faced with saying good-bye to loved ones. Leaving Roxbury had happened so fast there had been no time. Lone Wolf and the two young girls who had been giving me the gifts took my leaving the hardest. But after explaining to Lone Wolf my heart believed that my path led south, he accepted with little resistance. Several times, Lone Wolf's actions and questions hinted that he might like to go. I had learned in my time here that it was proper to wait to be asked for something rather than impose upon another.

He likely would have come if asked because I had saved his life. His companionship was not in my long-term plan and it wasn't clear if leaving the Wyandot behind was even in my best interest. I never asked him to go. He made it his mission to be by my side through every preparation to leave. These people were used to loss and always took it in stride. In the end, there were many thanks, there were a few tears, and some firm embraces but there was tremendous support for my choice as the right one. There would be lots of time for me to regret the decision to leave later.

BOOK 3

The French

Early French settlement took place in what is now Canada around present day Montreal and Quebec. The French colonial economy was built around the fur trade. French colonies in the New World grew very slowly at first compared to their English and Spanish rivals. This slow growth was due primarily to a challenging climate and corruption in the colonial government. Eventually French fur trappers traveled west and south to the areas north of The Great Lakes. Missions (religious settlements run by holy men) *were established throughout the region to convert Wyandot* (Huron to the French) *Native American Indian tribes to Christianity. By the late 1600s, trappers and missionaries pushed southward into the Ohio and Mississippi River valleys slowly making their way south to establish the present day city of New Orleans. Some holy men had success, while others met their death. Native American Indians often tolerated the French priests until they began to push too hard and disrupt their way of life too much. Huron enemies such as the Iroquois tribes also added to the danger. French fur trappers often met with greater success than missionaries and other European settlers in forging relationships with Native American Indian tribes. Many French fur trappers became self-sufficient and adopted aspects of Native American Indian culture to survive in the wild. They likely gained respect because of their ability to adapt and survive off of the land. They traded frequently in the villages of Algonquin and Huron tribes. Some spent winters with tribes they had befriended and even took Native American wives. Tribes that were depleted by sickness or conflict with rivals supported the practice. The French and the English eventually began to travel and trade for furs in the same areas. Conflict over trade in western parts of present day New York, Pennsylvania, and southward all the way to the Mississippi River were common. By the 1760s, their close ties to opposing Native American Indian tribes would lead to war between the two European powers and their allies. The French and Indian War, the North American theatre of the worldwide Seven Year's War, led to the loss of French control of North American territories.*

The French Way

Chapter 11

Jean-Luc Lalonde and Claude Fortin spoke both French and English. They displayed not a moment's hesitation concerning my addition to their travel party. We had become acquainted throughout the winter months and they seemed to respect my standing in the Wyandot tribe. Jean-Luc explained what materials would be needed. My Wyandot family helped me acquire each item in haste. We left the camp in the canoe I had built with my own hands, the one that had earned me the Wyandot name Tseeyee. The village disappeared quickly behind the dense foliage. After a short time, the river began to widen and the unsettled expanse of forests unfolded before our eyes on either side of the river. A feeling of peace descended upon me as the rhythmic paddling echoed from the distant shores. Wordless hours passed as we calmly embraced the serenity of the nature surrounding us. The seemingly endless network of streams and rivers provided for days of safe passage to the southwest.

Each day as dusk approached, we paddled to shore and found a place to set up camp. We would hastily gather dry wood for a fire and spend the spring evenings laying plans and exchanging stories while we enjoyed recently killed game or delved into our supply of dried foods. Jean-Luc and Claude shared many stories of their homeland and experiences since coming to the New World. They felt blessed to travel these majestic lands uninhibited by the laws and corruption of the colonial government in New France. Leaders of the city controlled all trade in and out of the city. They lined their pockets at the expense of the hard-working trappers who traveled the area surronding the massive lakes. Like many trappers, they preferred to do their business with the Wyandot and missions established by French priests avoiding direct contact with officials. During these peaceful evenings, bonds were strengthened be-tween friends and decisions were made about the journey ahead.

We would travel between two giant lakes to the south and return to the missions to trade when the burden of pelts became too great. Our path would eventually take us southward. The lessons learned in my time with the Wyandot served me well. To my delight, some of the skills acquired from my Wyandot brothers and sisters were new to the Frenchmen. It brought great satisfaction to be a contributor, as my new friends and I learned from each other during our travels. These men were tremendously resourceful in the deep wilderness. The wilderness was home. Out of respect, they mostly spoke English in my presence. However, each began to patiently teach me the French lan-guage during idle time. Within a few weeks we could have simple exchanges in French, which seemed to please them greatly.

Reaching the shores of the lake called the Lac de St. Louis (Ontario by the Indians) brought great joy to my companions. Jean-Luc produced a bottle of rum from his supplies that we passed around in celebration. They explained that the streams and inlets off of this great lake would provide us with bountiful beaver pelts for trade. We had many encounters with other trappers. Some were French but we also encountered various tribes of Indian trappers. They had cautioned me to allow them to do all of the talking in either case.

"How old are you young Silas?" Claude asked one star-filled early summer evening on the shores of this massive lake.

I hesitated in response, not out of secrecy but out of ignorance. "It depends on the current date," I replied a little embarrassed and feeling less informed than my companion.

Claude seemed to be thinking this over which put me at ease. After a bit of thought he responded, "My best calculations put us in late June, the year Sixteen hundred and fifty one." Jean-Luc was listening to this exchange with a look of curiosity.

"That would make me seventeen years and then some," I responded with an air of confidence. Both men nodded with what seemed to be approval. Neither spoke again for several minutes. This was not out of character. They often digested information slowly and thoughtfully before continuing conversation, similar and perhaps influenced by the Wyandot we had all spent so much time with.

"You are a worldly lad at your age," Claude offered. "Would it surprise you to know that I have a beauty of a wife by name of Marie de Montreal in New France?" This was a shocking admission to me considering the knowledge that both men had Native American wives in the Wyandot village. I couldn't help thinking how my parents would react to such a sinful admission.

Before I could respond Jean-Luc prodded Claude playfully. "Now if your purpose tonight is to spill out your soul to our young ami (friend), then complete honesty should accompany your confession. Beautiful may be off of the truth; perhaps you should try a description more like godly or friendly." To this Claude spit the swig of rum he had just taken into the fire and burst into raucous laughter.

"D'accord, or…alright!" Claude conceded, "Compared to the Huron princesses she has shortcomings. My purpose is to come clean and explain to our young friend our sinful behavior. Would the savages accept us winter after winter if we didn't prove our sincerity by living with their own? If we didn't show our abilities as providers and a willingness to accept their ways we might end up in one of the huts in that graveyard."

"Can't say I ever considered that deeply about it," Jean-Luc admitted with a thoughtful look, "It's just a better way to spend the winter than in a small cabin with you and your stench," he continued with a chuckle. "Why don't you tell Silas more about this French une femme (wife) you're bragging about?"

Claude smiled broadly as he continued, "Walking on the streets of the capital city, looking at the goods sold in them shops, I spied her through…"

"No, No, No!" Jean Luc interrupted loudly. "How long did you know your lady before being married? What's her last name? The good parts of it, not the whole boring story!"

"Well you know that week with her before we married was the happiest of my life," Claude snorted. "And just cause I don't recall her last name and use instead the name of the city where our love bloomed don't mean we are not true," he protested.

"Imagine it Silas, they met, married, and he left her all within a week. Not to mention the fool hasn't been back to see her for over two years now. I can't wait to get back there just to see if the pair even remembers what the other looks like. They'll likely walk right by each other and keep going," Jean-Luc teased. "What about you, Silas? There were rumors a couple of the tribal squaws had their *peepers* on you. But you up and fled with us before acting on it."

The two men stared at me with genuine interest. They clearly expected some kind of an explanation.

I drew a deep breath and began, "I once knew the most beautiful and witty girl..." I told them the whole story, about the first day we ever spoke and how Abigail materialized magically nearly everywhere for years. How she came from a family that was above mine, and the problem that created in English Puritan society despite how people felt about each other. How she flirted and that she was my best friend. Then I shared the story about her sister's death, the betrayal, and my arrest. It felt good to put the story to words for someone who came from similar culture. The story concluded with the last time I saw her crying in the clearing while fleeing. The words she appeared to mouth across the pond before I disappeared into the woods. The telling of the story had become more about my needs than those of the audience. The telling had brought me temporarily into a dreamlike state remembering vivid details like the wisdom in her eyes, the softness of her skin, or the smell of her hair. Coming back to my senses, I glanced across the fire at my companions. Both seemed to have been impacted deeply by the story. They had glossed over eyes and a faraway look as they drifted through their own memories, possibly of lost loves.

Another minute passed before Jean-Luc asked in a distant and seemingly far off tone, "Do you love her still?"

"I don't think I will ever have a choice," I responded thoughtfully.

Reflecting about the discussion later, I thought about Claude calling the Wyandot, who were so accepting and kind to us, savages. Briefly there was a pull inside of me that made me wonder if my loyalty to the people who had been so good to me had been challenged. It seemed it would be foolish to take offense to this lighthearted discussion. Especially considering how kind and sharing these two men had been since leaving the village two months earlier. It became clear that both men tolerated the Indians, but just as the people in the English settlement I grew up in viewed them as inferior; so did my French companions. Both men were enthralled by the Abigail story and frequently asked for the tale to be repeated on other starlit nights.

Chapter 12

We traveled along the coastline of this massive lake. It smelled and looked more like the Atlantic Ocean near my childhood village than any other lake I had ever seen. About one week later, we paddled up a small river and arrived at a mission, built between a fork in the river, as darkness approached. A great wall made from the trunks of trees surrounded the mission. Smoke drifted into the sky from multiple fires inside the enclosed settlement. A hill rose up behind the wall providing a backdrop of forest when viewing on approach from the river. On either side of the mission crops grew in well-attended fields. On one side, sparse feeble maize swayed gently in the evening breeze. The other field appeared to host a variety of local vegetables. The sky behind glowed orange, purple, and pink in the direction of the mountains as the daylight faded. There was only one entrance to the mission. Two large doors that swung outward.

A lookout gave word to open the gates before my companions had even spoken. Once inside, both Jean-Luc and Claude were greeted with handshakes and shoulder clasps by the mission residents. They spoke in French throughout introductions and the group that had greeted us welcomed me kindly. Toward the back of the settlement, in the direction of the hills, was a simple but tall church. The church tower stretched high into the sky and was crowned by a large cross. Smaller structures were built on both sides of the church. These appeared to house the Frenchmen who lived in the settlement. The center of the mission was clear. Built around the clearing close to the wall were 1520 homes made from the trunks of small trees and covered with multiple layers of bark from large trees. The Frenchmen called these structures *wigwams*.

We spent the next two days at the mission. We were given lodging in the building to the right of the church with the common French settlers. The building on the left was meant for the men of the church. We ate and traded our furs for supplies such as new knives, new traps, venison jerky, tobacco, and items of clothing to replace those that were wearing out. My companions seemed to hold a meeting with everyone of importance in the settlement and were gathering all the news and information they could before we moved on. It was amazing to see white settlers and Indians living together peacefully. There was something strange about these Native people adapting to white ways at a settlement far into the western world beyond white civilization. In territory that was theirs. These were Christian Indians but they were Wyandot, and after my experience with the Bear Clan I found the whole transformation confusing. I felt confident the Wyandot of Lone Wolf would never accept this type of change. They respected and loved their traditions so much. But clearly this Wyandot Clan had changed and they could not have been that different from the Bear Clan.

Jean-Luc, Claude, and I sat down after supper the second day and had a long discussion. It was the first time they had sought my input into planning our next move. They provided information that they had learned through discussions with the leaders of the mission. There had been a lot of talk about "great rivers" to the south that no white man had ever seen. There was a great land bridge between Lac de St. Louis and another great lake that led to very dangerous Seneca Indian territory. The natives spoke of a great mountain range to the southeast of Seneca territory. The streams that came out of these mountains were home to the finest furs the Indians had ever seen. To the east of these mountains, lived white men who the natives in the region felt were *very* dangerous. They claimed that they were spreading over the land and carried sickness in them that easily spread. I shared with them that this could be the colonies of Virginia settled by the English or even the rumored Dutch settlements. To the west of the mountains, they warned of tribes that hated these white men because they had forced them to leave their lands. Both of my companions agreed we had about four months left before the onset of winter. Despite the danger, they were considering heading south to these mountains and spending some time trapping. After briefly exploring and trapping, they would head back to this mission for the winter unless a better opportunity presented itself.

Jean Luc shifted his eyes away from the stick he had been poking into the dirt and looked firmly into my eyes. "Silas, this could be a mighty dangerous journey. There would be no shame in staying behind and waiting for our return." Claude nodded his head in support of his friend.

A smile slowly began to form on my lips in response to the seriousness of his tone. Both men looked to be confused by this reaction. "Considering my main reason for joining the two of you was to make my way to Virginia, and the fact that danger has been a constant companion for over a year, the excitement offered by this adventure seems nearly irresistible."

Both men happily accepted this explanation. Claude slapped his leg and snorted, "I told you he's a brave one and wouldn't let old Lalond and Fortin go off on our own."

Claude's enthusiasm was rewarding. A feeling of acceptance rushed over me. We were in this together and we valued each other mutually. After my arrest in Roxbury and the way my parents had betrayed me, no matter how comfortable a situation appeared doubts always floated around in my mind. It felt good to trust my partners.

Chapter 13

We could not have been more wrong about our first trip south to the eastern mountains of the continent. We traveled the foothills of those mountains for a month after the long journey there and encountered not one soul. We saw evidence of Indian tribes, but were careful to avoid contact. The trapping was excellent and my education as a fur trapper continued. The lands we encountered inspired a peace in me never felt before. The rolling hills and raging streams that flowed from the eastern mountains strangely inspired a feeling of welcome. The belief that this would be or was supposed to be home grew with each passing day. Once as a child, my brother Micah and I were learning to hunt deep in the woods from my father. Father came to a clearing and stopped. He looked up into the high pine, oak, and maple trees that surrounded us. Staring up and slowly spinning he instructed us to listen carefully. "Do you hear it?" he asked in a pleading tone. "Do either of you?" He continued almost desperate now, as he still looked skyward. I snuck a peak from the corner of one eye at Micah, who stood next to Father staring upward with a look of recognition. Father continued, "As a boy in England, I stood in several great churches and looked up at the high ceilings with the beautiful artwork all around and heard music. That's the closest to heaven I have ever felt. But sometimes when the woods are still and quiet and I look up at the beauty of God's creation here in the deep woods, I hear that same music and feel close to heaven like in those childhood moments." As soon as he paused, my brother burst in, "I hear it Father!" he exclaimed excitedly. I heard nothing. To please Father I echoed my brother's words. Traveling with Jean-Luc and Claude through these unsettled lands, the urge to stop frequently and look up was uncontrollable. I heard music, and it was beautiful, instinctively I knew this was home.

The return trip to the mission was equally peaceful. We all agreed long before returning to the mission that we would be heading back to the southern mountains again in the spring. The last couple of weeks before reaching the mission turned dreadfully cold. The excitement that arose in me as we laid eyes on our winter home was barely containable. Just as quickly, an eerie coldness began to engulf my limbs producing a tingly sensation. The feel of blood flowing through a network of veins was recognizable as the chills led to uncontrollable shudders seizing my body. The first warning sign was the absence of the smoke from fires I had seen the first time we approached the mission. Second, there were no guards and the large gate was open with the wooden door splintered. I could see the cross of the church rising above the settlement walls and there was a large black bird sitting ominously on top of the cross. Before we even stepped inside there was a perceivable odor and strange sounds that indicated something was wrong. The smell of death filled the air. The cackle of birds and the snarling of some predators were audible as we came near the door. Even the most hardened men could not have been prepared for the grisly sight we stepped into. Flashbacks of the dead Wyandot on the canoes, a year earlier, immediately raced into my mind. Surveying the interior of the mission there were rotting, decaying, half-eaten corpses everywhere. The Frenchmen we had stayed with, the holy men my companions had held conference with, and members of the Wyandot Deer Clan lay dead and scattered. Coyotes and wild dogs fought for scraps of flesh and ravenous crows sat perched all over, pecking at the desecrated bodies. Most of the buildings had been at least partially burned. Upon inspection, it became clear another Native American tribe had slaughtered them. Most bodies were littered with arrows or had skulls that had been crushed by either a club or a tomahawk. A few of the priests had been tied to posts in front of the church and burned to death. Their blackened, charred bodies were crumpled at the base of each post, falling only after the ropes that held them had burnt. They were likely burned in protest of the changes they tried to impose on the Native Americans of the region. A flood of emotions overwhelmed the three of us. We were devastated by the savagery of the attack, the loss of anticipated companions, and the recognition of the new challenges we'd face. The next several days were spent silently cleaning up the massacre. The bodies were buried, gate repaired, and most of the buildings demolished to acquire enough salvageable materials to repair and rebuild the least damaged shelter. We searched the mission and the nearby fields for any food that had not been taken or destroyed. It was not a shock that very little had been left behind by the raiders. Immediate efforts to fish and hunt began. Results were poor due to the previous onset of cold weather. We dried the little meat we acquired before the arrival of full winter.

The winter was difficult, but we proved resourceful enough to survive. Never before had I experienced the pangs of hunger to such a degree. The spasms of pain that grip your stomach due to lack of food were nearly unbearable at times. As months passed, the situation grew more desperate. By late winter, Claude and Jean-Luc began to collect tree bark and insist we all chew on bark and leather clothing for several hours each day. We spent long days repairing traps, making new clothing, and inventing projects to distract from the pains brought by hunger. We retold stories that by the end of winter all three could now recite word for word. Claude religiously carved markings onto the wall of the shelter to represent each day. We anxiously awaited any sign of spring. Much time was spent debating new plans for the coming season. We needed to travel either north or west to trade the furs we had trapped. Certain supplies were necessary to head back to the southeastern mountains. Claude and Jean-Luc knew where to go, but were fearful of finding only devastation or deserted villages. Even our Bear Clan companions from the previous winter had uprooted and moved northeast. It was very likely this was a practice being copied by other clans and villages.

In the end, come spring, we agreed to head west because it didn't take us as far out of the intended path. This decision proved to be extremely lucky. The weather finally broke. After traveling northwest only one day out of the way, we encountered a group of Wyandot Wolf Clan migrating northeast to escape Haudenosaunee (Iroquois) raids. The same decision the Bear Clan had made the previous spring. They were able to provide for most of our needs through trade. For a day, stories were exchanged between our two groups. The increasing violence and aggression of the rival Indians dominated the talks. The next day, resupplied and rejuvenated, we walked anxiously away from the Wolf Clan party to resume our journey. The southeastern mountains were the desired destination.

Chapter 14

It had been nearly two years since leaving Roxbury. Frequently I fantasized about a return to Roxbury. Not a permanent return, just a chance to see mother, Abigail, and even my brother Micah. Would these people that I left behind even know me? Not that my appearance was much different. My brown hair was now long and braided in the style of my Wyandot brothers. Patches of hair grew on a poorly groomed face. But would they see other changes by looking into my hardened brown eyes? I left Roxbury a boy. Luck allowed for survival those first days in the woods after my escape. Survival no longer depended on luck. The vast knowledge gained through my time with the Wyandot and French companions had transformed me into a self-sufficient man. A smile came to my lips as I remembered how important the meaning of our names had been to my mother. Spending time in the woods as a boy had given me a sense of pride because of that knowledge. How naïve it had been to think I understood the forest then. What would mother think of her son now? The son who had become what mother had taught in innocent childhood lessons. A son that had become what he was destined to be. A "man of the woods" as my name stood for.

We traveled south at a slow pace due to intentional caution. We were very concerned about having any kind of contact with the tribes of the Seneca. Many stories had been told to my companions about their hatred of the French. They were likely the ones that had destroyed the mission. Once we passed through this territory, based on our trip the previous year, we were confident safe conditions would await us. There had been little evidence of an Indian presence once we had reached the mountain region.

The experience we had in the mountains mirrored that of the first trip early on. We saw some of the most beautiful scenery any of us could recall ever encountering. One day early in the summer, we came into a clearing in the middle of the mountains that was filled with large rocks. It was the most majestic sight any of us had ever seen. It was a field of large rocks as wide as a river and at least as long as a village. There were no trees in the field. We skipped from rock to rock marveling at the piled field of stones.

The various pelts were plentiful in the mountain ponds and streams. We continued moving south for the next few weeks traveling west away from the higher peaks and into the foothills area. We sometimes followed rivers for long distances into the mountains or hills until we came to a place narrow enough to pass. The weather became extremely warm for a stretch in midsummer. We headed east hoping to find a cooler climate in the mountains. It was on this trek that we accidentally came into contact with a band of Susquehannock Indians. Great care was taken to avoid contact with all Indians. The presence of groups in an area was usually discovered through signs we detected early. So avoidance was usually easy. But while following a stream in a hilly region one day we approached a large waterfall. Anxious to drink and bathe in the cool water we moved excitedly toward the base of the waterfall. The sound of the flowing water was just loud enough to allow us to walk right into the midst of a hunting party with a dozen braves. A few bathed in the large pool at the base of the cascading water. Many were already staring at us as we entered the clearing. None made a move. They only stared at us curiously. Jean-Luc, whom both Claude and I looked to as our leader, was the first to speak. Tribes of the northeast spoke many different dialects of the Iroquoian language. The conversation that took place was surprisingly easy for me to follow. Most of the words were recognizable. It was impressive to see Jean-Luc navigate his way through the conversation with relative ease. At first, Jean-Luc was asking many questions to gain information. Eventually, he began telling them the story of the mission and the difficult winter we had there. Luckily, the Susquehannock were a tribe that was not hostile to Europeans like us. Jean-Luc even managed to exchange some of our furs for much needed supplies before we were allowed to pass.

That evening after setting up camp, we discussed the information they had shared. The Susquehannock and the southern Lenape clans shared the territory we were traveling in. The Susquehannock and the Haudennosaunee were bitter enemies and frequently raided one another. The Lenape tribes had moved west after conflict with the eastern English and Dutch settlers. The Lenape hated these settlers for stealing their land. There were rumors that some of the Lenape took the eastern white men prisoner and traveled south to trade them to the Spanish. The Spanish were said to offer huge rewards for English settlers. Jean-Luc seemed to think because Claude and I had stayed silent the Indians we encountered believed us to all be French. As we settled on our beaver fur blankets to sleep that night, Jean-Luc and Claude continued to speak quietly as I drifted off.

Three days later, we began to suspect we were being followed. The forest did not sound right. After some debate, we decided to do a large circle with the intention of crossing our own path to look for evidence of pursuit. Before we had a chance to complete this plan, we were confronted by a group of Indians that looked different from the group seen days before. It was immediately clear that this band had different intentions. Their weapons were drawn and their glares displayed fierceness. They were dressed as warriors and were covered in bright colored paints. Their skin was darker than the others we had interacted with. Many wore arm and leg bands made of what appeared to be silver and gold. Jean-Luc instructed Claude and I to place our weapons on the ground. A moment's hesitation served only to confirm that we were surrounded. Jean-Luc spoke to two of the Indians (only later was it clarified that they were southern Lenape). Both he and the Indians spoke more slowly than the conversation a few days before. There were fewer recognizable words. After a few minutes, without turning to face us, Jean-Luc instructed Claude and me to introduce ourselves and tell where we came from. The conversation between Jean-Luc and the leader of the group continued again after we had both spoken.

Eventually, I felt relieved to see Jean-Luc and the warriors he spoke with all nod and come to some sort of an agreement. But as Jean-Luc turned around it was clear something had gone wrong. His face was pale. His expression as he looked at me seemed to display a mixture of horror and apology. I glanced to Claude who stood at my side. He was staring at the ground and refused to look up or speak even when I murmured, "Claude?" Jean-Luc approached in three slow strides. He interrupted as I attempted to question what was happening. "Silas, these are Lenape Indians of the Turkey Clan. You must go with them now. They intend to take you far south. There are men there that are trading generously for English prisoners. I am sorry." His eyes showed that he was sincere.

Anger rose from deep inside as my temple throbbed at the recognition of betrayal. Their hushed tones at the fire days earlier now made sense. They had realized this possibility existed and they had planned for it. Both men gathered their weapons without making further eye contact and walked to the north without looking back. The words he spoke were eerily familiar to those father had spoken years before on the day I was taken prisoner in Roxbury. A feeling of wonder rushed in bringing the question of whether God was punishing me for those past sins.

BOOK 4

The Spanish

The Spanish and Portuguese were the first two European countries to compete for land in the New World after the voyages of Christopher Columbus. Early settlement was focused in South America and the many scattered islands in the Atlantic Ocean centrally located off the coast of North and South America. Spanish Conquistadors successfully routed Native American Indian empires such as the Aztec and Inca in their search for gold and resources. The Spanish established the first permanent European colony in North America at St. Augustine, Florida in 1565. Slowly, and mostly unsuccessfully, the Spanish built missions as they tried to expand their presence in the area around and north of St. Augustine for the next 250 years. English colonization in North America, beginning in the early 1600s with the settlement of Jamestown, Virginia, eventually led to conflict with the Spanish settlers by the mid 1600s. Spanish missions were settled as far north as present day North Carolina to convert local Native American tribes to Christianity and provide food for St. Augustine. In the mid 1600s, English *expansion and slave raids led to conflict with these same tribes. The Spanish eventually established **garrisons** in most provinces to deal with the problem. Over time, Spanish colonial leaders called for missions to retreat toward St. Augustine or coastal areas to be more easily protected. The English established additional colonies throughout the 1700s taking control of the region with the exception of Florida, which remained a Spanish possession until 1819 when the land was purchased by The United States from Spain.*

The Spanish Way

Chapter 15

Two Lenape warriors bound my hands using a leather strap. The strap was tied firmly around each wrist with two or less inches of slack in between. Clearly the design would put me at a disadvantage if I chose to fight for my freedom. They didn't seem very concerned about me making that choice. They were very organized. My bonds were checked and tightened several times a day. They rotated guard shift and other responsibilities in groups of two whenever we stopped. We moved south at a very rapid pace for over two weeks. We camped each night from dark until sunrise. Only twice, the second and third day after I was captured, did we stop for longer than a brief break during the day. Each time one half of the dozen well-armed warriors left and after an hour or two returned with another captive. The first time this happened the other captive and I were given a firm speech by one of the warriors. Only some words were recognizable to me. It seemed best to keep silent but neither of us knew what he was trying to communicate. Moments later we began our march. The new captive began to speak quietly asking for my name and village. With lightening quickness we were both brutally beaten by several of our captors. As we lay bloodied and winded from savage blows, it was now clear the instructions had to do with us not speaking. The brief exchange had at least clarified that the new prisoner was also English. When the next captive came into camp and the same speech was given, we both held our index finger to our lips to save the new captive from suffering the beating we had received the previous day.

Escape would be impossible. These lands were foreign and the Lenape were clearly excellent trackers. A failed escape attempt would likely result in death. We clearly had some value to them and killing us was not their intention. Having accepted these facts, I spent the long days of silent travel reflecting on the past and speculating about our destination. Feelings of betrayal and disappointment in friends and loved ones dominated these thoughts. But now, exhausted from days of travel and unsure of the dreadful fate that waited for me in some mysterious destination, beliefs of wrongdoing were being called into question. Who was I? Did I ever accept blame for actions? Had I ever been truthful with myself or was I too selfish and stubborn? Had I ever considered the danger I put my family and Abigail in with my actions and words in Roxbury? Why had I broken into the house in the clearing that night, instead of knocking on the door the next morning and asking the family for what I needed? Hadn't I left my Wyandot family that had taught me so much and cared for me as their own with little consideration for anyone but myself? Only now did I admit to myself that Jean-Luc and Claude had not betrayed me. They had acted out of self-preservation. Trying to save me likely would have cost them their own freedom or even their lives. Perhaps a feeling of self-pity brought on by uncertainty about the future, contributed to the decision I made that day. A decision to promise God and myself that if he saw fit to bring me out of this ordeal alive, all my future decisions would always take into consideration the well-being of everyone involved. A vow made to see the world and each situation as the man I had become and not the boy from the past.

After two weeks of travel southward, my fellow captives and I were in terrible condition. Limited food and constant movement were beginning to show on our haggard faces. The injuries sustained after speaking to the other prisoner days earlier were also contributing to our deteriorating condition. Despite the challenges, I became resolved to hide the pain and be as cooperative as possible. The other captives seemed to follow my lead while traveling and when camped. Without the luxury of words to support and encourage them, actions and determination would have to suffice. The other two captives most likely had less knowledge of the situation we were facing. There was a destination at the end of this long path and I was certain the purpose was not our death, at least not immediately. Near the end of the third week of travel, shortly after crossing a shallow river, the other prisoner who had been beaten for speaking to me passed out and fell violently face first to the forest floor. Cautiously, I came to a stop. The other prisoner followed my lead and came to a halt as well. Rather than rush to the fallen man's aid, I held out my bound hands palms up and looked to our captors for permission to act. One of the two warriors we had come to recognize as the leaders gave me a quick nod and soft grunt of approval. Calmly we proceeded to our fallen comrade's side. We were unable to revive him but the feel of his soft breaths on my fingers and cheek confirmed he was alive. Wordlessly we propped him up and attempted to raise the slackened body. Bound hands made it impossible to carry him no matter what position we tried. Out of frustration one of the Lenape leaders drew a knife, a European knife, and advanced quickly toward us.

As he approached, I closed my eyes anticipating the end of our fallen companion's life. There was a brief tug and a moment's confusion before the realization that the leather that had bound my hands had been cut. Free of restraints, we carried the fallen man for the next two days with blind determination. Luckily, because all three of us likely would not have made it another day, we reached a place called San Luis de Inhayea at the end of the second day.

Our exhaustion was so great that we collapsed to the ground immediately. We realized the destination of our long days of travel had been reached. It was a struggle to see through tear-streaked eyes, as the world around seemed to waver from side to side despite my best efforts to focus. The voices of the Lenape and what sounded like others speaking neither English nor French were audible. Despite never having heard the language before, I presumed that the other voices were speaking Spanish. Some of the words were similar to the French language. The men spoke so fast there was no chance of following the discussion. Recollection of the exchange was spotty in my memory, but before passing out completely it appeared the Lenape Indians were provided with numerous supplies in trade for us, including guns.

Chapter 16

My eyes opened briefly from time to time but it was impossible to bring anything into focus. Dreams occupied my semi-conscious mind for long stretches of time. Mother and Father were there. Micah, Abigail, Reverend Washburn, Amos Perkins, Lone Wolf, Claude, and Jean-Luc all made appearances. Events from my past were relived in these dreams and at times people made appearances in settings where they had never existed. One dream came to me many times.

Abigail sat at a small table in an unfamiliar log cabin. I entered happy to see her smile and smelled the freshly baked bread. Her face glowed with feelings of pride. She held a newborn baby up to me and she whispered, "There's your papa." Her skin appeared illuminated and a golden hue surrounded her making her appear to be angelic. She then stood and glided across the earthen floor. She slides her small soft hand inside of my rough and calloused one and we seemingly floated out the door and across the small clearing in front of the home. We continued floating over the field full of crops and eventually come to a stop in the forest beyond. Music filled my ears and I recognized the place in the hills from my first trip south with Jean-Luc and Claude. Abigail stares lovingly into my eyes as her beauty and the look of joy in her face instill in me a feeling of internal peace. Her lips part and she speaks her words softly, "Keep going Silas," she pleads.

After several days drifting in and out of consciousness, I regained my senses and found I was inside of a small church. Two other men also lay on blankets in a corner of the room near me. Benches fill the center of the room and a raised platform with a wooden stand serves as a *pulpit*. A statue of Jesus crucified on the cross hangs on the wall behind the wooden stand. One of the men is the fellow captive I helped carry the last two days of the journey to this location. He is smiling at me. "We were beginning to worry you wouldn't come around. According to Henry, our other traveling companion, you saved my life," he says. "My name is John, John Quick. We are now captives of a Spanish garrison that is rebuilding a mission called San Luis. The Spanish have been rewarding Indians well for English captives. Apparently some Englishmen have been responsible for Indian slave raids that have brought trouble for the Spanish in these parts," he explains quietly. Two priests were now staring at us from across the room. "I'm sorry to throw this all upon you in your current state, but moments for us to speak undisturbed have been infrequent. We have been brought here as slave laborers to help build the new mission. There are currently at least seven other Englishmen here besides us." One of the priests approached with a bowl of venison stew. He spoke to us in Spanish and then fed me with care. I was so famished the meal tasted like one of the best of my life. John Quick and the other injured man went to work the next day. I was alone in the church for two more days before going to work with the others.

We built buildings, walls, trenches, and cleared fields during the day. We weren't overworked. The priests would not allow it. In the evenings, we were put into a small storage shed after the evening meal. The crowded shed had two levels of wooden shelves built onto each side wall that served as beds. There were enough shackles and spaces to hold ten prisoners. Each man had one wrist placed into a shackle that was attached to a chain anchored into the floorboards or ceiling. This allowed access to a small space occupied by the wooden platforms and a blanket. A guard was posted at each end of the structure at all times. This would be our life for the next two years. Once healthy, I went about the work with pride and maximum effort. After considering the position of the Spanish guards, it seemed best to accept that they were just doing their job. It was made easier by the fact that almost all guards treated us well if we cooperated. Fortunately, this approach led me to good relations with many of the Spanish soldiers. Having already been taught the French language, learning to speak Spanish came easily.

The most difficult part of those two years for me wasn't the labor or the Spanish guards. Unfortunately, this was not the case for many fellow prisoners. Many had left behind wives and children. They were unsure of the fate that had befallen their loved ones. They couldn't accept the position we were in. Despite my best efforts to encourage their patience, some broke down both physically and mentally and a few even attempted escape. They were my daily companions and inevitably we developed close bonds. It was easy to care about them but necessary for me to keep them at a distance emotionally. Henry Wheaton, who had carried John Quick into the mission settlement with me, died six months after we arrived in an escape attempt. He was shot through the eye by a guard and his body was left in front of our sleeping shed for two days as a warning. Some unknown predator dragged his corpse away the second night. John Quick died of illness after a year and a half. It was not uncommon for several prisoners to become sick. New prisoners arrived from time to time at the settlement over the two years. We never had more than fourteen in the settlement and never fewer than seven.

Despite my young age, both fellow prisoners and the Spanish guards came to view me as the leader of the prisoners. This respect was likely granted due to a combination of my survival skills, cooperative attitude, and ability to converse in English, French, Native American tongues, and Spanish. My understanding of Spanish and local Indian languages grew steadily. The dialect spoken by local tribes was different but some words were similar making it easy to begin picking up the meanings of other words. When the Spanish guards were becoming concerned about the behavior or mental state of a fellow prisoner they would call on me to help solve their problem. By counseling the prisoner in question or issuing a stern warning, the arrangement was mostly successful. However, even the guards seemed to understand that some men could only be patient for so long before they had to take their chance at an escape to get back to those they had been taken away from. When patience ran out and these decisions were made I provided as much knowledge as possible to help the man with his attempt.

The best friend I made during this time was a Virginian named Daniel Wood. He was almost the same age as me. He had not yet taken a wife and had been taken prisoner shortly after moving from his father's land to begin creating his own homestead in western Virginia. His father had come to Virginia as an *indenture*. He had served his time in labor and eventually earned his freedom and land. Daniel was eager to learn. I spent free moment's teaching him the skills acquired in my travels. He shared stories of his upbringing in the Virginia territory. I was intensely curious about life in these settlements as compared to Roxbury. His stories and parts of stories from other Virginia prisoners began to bring on a feeling of concern. They spoke of a world that seemed full of sickness and death. They seemed to accept this as normal circumstance. Virginia seemed to be a place where ambitious young men fought for possession of land, status, and even women due to the disproportionate number of men and women. My curiosity about this place from earlier years began to fade. Daniel and the other prisoners were constantly asking me to repeat the stories of my previous adventures. Their admiration and interest brought on a sense of pride for the life I had lived the previous three years. Daniel became a true friend, but despite his loyalty, something deep inside warned me to keep him at a distance. While repairing the exterior wall on the east side of the mission settlement, just out of hearing from the guards assigned to us, he cautiously brought up a subject that had apparently been on his mind for a long time. "Silas, we have been here together as prisoners since my arrival close to a year ago. Not once have you brought up escape from this place. Every other captive here has talked to me of escape. All agree that you would have the best chance of success."

"Why do none speak to me of this?" I inquired.

"The...the men here respect you," he continued carefully, "but they are afraid because of your close relationship and many conversations with the guards. They don't understand you."

I thought on this for a moment before continuing. "To me Daniel, this is but another adventure to survive. These are hostile lands for us. Escape is unlikely and we are not treated horribly. The guards are men who have a job to do. Cooperation with them has served us all well as the rules and our freedoms around the mission over the months have become more relaxed. I have always considered escape and perhaps someday the opportunity will come when success is in my favor."

"The men will be happy to hear of this," he interrupted.

"Perhaps Daniel, it would be best if we kept this between us. Trust with the guards could never be restored if it were lost. If the time is ever right for escape I will know."

"Just promise me that if that time ever comes you will take me with you," he said with an air of desperation in his voice.

"I will do everything in my power to make it so, friend," I nodded to affirm my commitment though already aware this was not a promise I could guarantee.

Chapter 17

We never had the chance. One month later, the guards abruptly informed us our work in the mission settlement was done and we were being taken south to a garrison near the colony of St. Augustine. This colony was rumored to be the original Spanish settlement in these parts.

After the announcement was made, I was summoned to the soldier's quarters for a special meeting. A small group of soldiers were headed north and they needed a man with survival and interpreter skills to accompany them. The invitation was accepted without hesitation. Unsuccessfully, I tried to convince them to allow Daniel to accompany the exploration party as well. He had been a great student but they had no interest in two guides. It was difficult to accept not being able to help Daniel. We had become friends and there had been a promise made to try to help him. However, I was elated to be headed in the direction of my imagined future rather than heading further away. The guards gave me immediate quarter alone in a newer storage shed. The next morning the guards retrieved me for morning meal. The other prisoner sheds were eerily quiet. The other prisoners had already left for their southern destination. I never saw Daniel or any of the others again.

We traveled the lands for the next two years returning to San Luis only for the winter months. We were accompanied both years by a surveyor, named Gaspar Odalis, who mapped the lands. The first year there were also ten soldiers and a man of medicine they called Senor Pepito in the group. The main goal was to look for future mission and settlement sites. The first year the party originally headed west, but came to a great river that was a barrier to further travel in that direction due to the strong currents and vast width. Most of the time was spent closer to the mountain range, I suspected was the same one, I had visited years earlier with my French companions. This expedition was much farther south than the lands we had explored while fur trapping years earlier. Comandante Munoz was the leader. My role was quickly established as tracker, interpreter, hunter, and laborer. Whenever our band encountered other groups of European trappers or Indians, to the front I was marched to begin communications. When it came time to camp, many of the necessary set-up tasks were mine. It was a return to the lifestyle I had grown to love during the time spent with the Wyandot and then Jean-Luc and Claude. The soldiers were respectful but kept their distance at first. Comandante Munoz had a quick temper and angry demeanor with everyone but was believed to be fair.

A few months after leaving the settlement at San Luis, we faced the first of several difficulties that year. On a rain soaked, unseasonably cool, early summer day, in a hilly region, we were forced to cross a small ravine. The fast moving stream that had cut the ravine went on a long distance both north and south of our location. We found an area where the ravine was only about the length of a man across. There was a small landing area with an incline to the left and a steep drop to the right. Comandante Munoz ordered me to jump across to the landing area first. With limited thought about possible consequences, the task was completed successfully. Munoz followed without incident. As did four more soldiers in succession. Next up was a nervous looking Gaspar, the surveyor, who upon landing lost his footing and rolled helplessly to the right. He clawed at the rocky terrain desperately as he slid toward the steep embankment. Nobody moved to help. On instinct, I grabbed the rapier from the belt of the nearest soldier. After two long strides, I jammed the weapon into a crack close to the edge of the cliff and slid toward the horrified Gaspar, just as he slid off the landing over the edge of the cliff. Luckily the blade held securely as Gaspar latched onto my legs and held tight. Unfortunately, there was only room for my right hand on the sword handle so my left hand was badly cut when I grabbed the blade to keep us from falling to the depths below. Within seconds, the nearby soldiers were beginning to haul us both up and away from certain death. Munoz responded with a reward. He placed an order that allowed me to carry both a rapier and knife during the day as we traveled. This proved very fortunate for Maximo Faustino, one of the soldiers.

Three weeks later, peril reared its head again. We had stopped at a shallow, but fast moving stream in a wooded area for a drink. No one heard or saw the two bear cubs on the other side of the stream until they bound into the water directly across from us. Poor Maximo just happened to be closest to the cubs as mother bear burst through the thicket on the opposite side of the stream. Before he could even reach a weapon, the angry bear was upon him determined to protect her young. The bear went for his head but he thrust his arm forward into the bloodthirsty jaws as the bear latched on. The men closest to Maximo were scrambling away to safety. Again, on instinct, I did the opposite. The bear was over

Maximo, swinging its head and poor Maximo side to side violently, with its back to me. Sprinting forward, searching frantically, my good hand finally grasped the knife it was seeking. I jumped on the bear's back wrapping my legs tightly to the mid section of the bear. I threw my arms around the bear's neck. Just as the surprised bear released Maximo from its deadly jaws, I pulled the knife upwards toward the bear's throat with all my strength. Pain shot through my left hand and up the arm from the previous injury. There was a soft gasp and gurgle as warmth engulfed both hands before my body was launched violently through the air. The blue sky and thick forest rotated past before the stony ground took the breath from my helpless body. My mind was still sharp and fear of the bear's retaliation gripped me while lying powerless, breathless on the stream's bank. Moments later several soldiers appeared above in my line of vision. Some began cautiously helping me to my feet. One soldier raised my blood-soaked hands in the air and all cheered.

Maximo lay on the ground nearby being tended to by Senor Pepito, for the lacerations on his arm. The soldiers half carried me across the clearing to Maximo's side. The injured man thanked me in broken English, the first time I could recollect any Spanish soldier speaking the language, as tears of joy at being alive streamed down his face.

All the members of the expedition the first year treated me differently after those two events. They still took away the weapons I carried during the day when we set up camp, and shackled my feet when we lay down to sleep, but I was otherwise treated as a companion rather than a prisoner. Even Comandante Munoz began to display kindness in our interactions, at least most of the time. Everyone began to share the labor of camp set-up and breakdown.

Maximo Faustino, whose last name ironically means lucky, and I became close friends. We faced many dangers and tense encounters with Indians together. We shared the stories of our lives. He told me about the far off land, called Spain, across the ocean where he grew up. In some ways, it reminded me of stories my father had told of his life before he had crossed the ocean. The parts of Maximo's stories about the large cities and beautiful churches were especially familiar. I told him about my adventures and Roxbury where I grew up. After he recovered from the injuries, Maximo was always at my side. When we encountered Indians, he would accompany me forward to communicate bravely with the often unpredictable tribes. The Indians we encountered were almost always willing to trade for the many items we carried for that purpose, but asked many questions, clearly suspicious, about why the Spanish had come. I always responded that they only wished to learn about the land. Careful to avoid divulging plans to settle missions or introduce new religions. When questioned about the interactions by Comandante Munoz, I described the natives as simple people who seemed only concerned with what they could gain. He seemed satisfied with this. Only Maximo came to know about my time with the Wyandot. Only he came to understand how I really felt about these people that the rest viewed as savages.

In the early fall, after turning south and heading back to San Luis, sickness overtook the expedition. Most showed at least mild symptoms. Several of us were gravely ill. For several days it was a struggle to even walk, despite our pace having slowed to a crawl. Skull splitting pains drummed through the head, chills, weakness of the limbs, and fever had a crippling effect on the most unlucky of us. Finally Maximo, who suffered only minor discomfort, convinced Munoz to let him take over all of my labor. Munoz even held camp for the next five days allowing most to recover enough to continue. Those of us who were the most affected lay crippled during the seemingly endless days. There were moments when I began to feel that survival was unlikely. The dream of Abigail, in the forest cabin, from years before returned to bring on a feeling of calm in the darkest hour.

One soldier named Juanito Reyes succumbed to the sickness and was sadly buried in the lonely forest. Maximo, spooked by the death, insisted on doing my chores for several more days after we resumed our march to allow time for me to recover. The loyalty and bond between us continued to deepen.

Chapter 18

As the weather turned colder, we returned to San Luis. Munoz, Gaspar, Maximo, and I spent many days discussing and planning for a return to the northern lands the next spring. Being included in these strategy meetings pleased me greatly. Two other soldiers, new to San Luis, eventually began to attend these meetings as well. They came to be known to me as Cantos and Manuel. Both quietly digested information we shared at first. Eventually, both contributed and Cantos even became assertive and even quite outspoken. The news that none of the soldiers, except for Maximo, from the previous expedition was going in the coming spring was a disappointment to me. The impact this would have on me could never have been imagined. The seven new soldiers were from a regiment that Cantos had led for the last two years. This gave Cantos a high standing in the expedition, second only to Comandante Munoz. Cantos had attended less than a half dozen meetings before our first confrontation. Munoz was discussing travel north when he asked my opinion about sticking to the foothills region or trying to travel more quickly in the flat region to the west. My response was based on patterns the Frenchmen had taught about the best way to avoid contacts with Indian tribes. "Traveling in the foothills is more difficult but safer due..." Cantos interrupted in Spanish speaking quickly, making clear he was appalled. "How do we plan our mission on word of a prisoner with no experience with the Spanish army or likely any army? We let a coward tell us to avoid conflict with savages in land that our government rightfully owns by treaty granted by the pope many years ago." Munoz continued to look down at his maps for at least ten seconds and only spoke when Cantos tried to continue. "I am of the opinion that this prisoner has proved to be loyal and possesses knowledge and skills that will serve us all well on expedition. There is no doubt in my mind given time you will all see this as well." Cantos was clear to all even before we left that he did not like nor understand my role in planning the expedition or the respect that the other men afforded me.

Provisions were gathered as soon as the weather broke. In less than a week, it was clear this trip would be much different from the previous year's adventure. Cantos and his men were quarrelsome and confrontational with the returning men and each other. Maximo overheard Cantos arguing frequently with Munoz over my position and privileges. Maximo warned me to stay close to him and shared rumors he had heard about Cantos' cruelty to prisoners and soldiers under his command. Unlike the previous year, camp life was miserable for all. Only Maximo provided me with help around camp. Cantos and the new soldiers took pleasure in ordering me to do meaningless small tasks. Most of the time the men complained about their assignment, rather than enjoying any aspect of the land or expedition we were on. They claimed that my lack of restraints and carrying weapons on the trail put them all in danger.

Still, Munoz refused to change his policies with regards to my privileges.

After failing to get his way, Cantos began attempts to sabotage my standing with Comandante Munoz. He first accused me of stealing food. Munoz dismissed the charge casually explaining that if I wanted extra food I would simply shoot extra game while hunting. He also reminded Cantos that the prisoner he so often attacked secured a large portion of the game for the whole company. Next, he claimed that many soldiers were complaining that I constantly confronted them and challenged their authority. To this, Munoz laughed and explained that in over three years he had never heard me speak unless giving helpful advice or answering a question. He even lectured Cantos on how I had constantly helped them with unruly prisoners during the building of San Luis whenever asked. Cantos never quit over the warm summer months. He finally accused me of trying to sabotage the whole expedition during an exchange with a dangerous looking band of Indians.

He claimed to have some knowledge of their language. He asked that Munoz allow him to properly punish me with lashes. Munoz angrily denied his request explaining that he couldn't count on his fingers the number of times my interpreter skills had saved his life. However, he did offer to let Cantos take over the job of being first to speak with tribes we encountered. Cantos quickly backed off. Edmundo Cantos was not a man who could live with his judgment and authority being questioned. His hatred of me grew. I stayed close to either Maximo or Munoz at all times. Cantos watched me like a predator observes its prey before striking. On a rainy late summer day, he finally saw his opportunity.

Munoz, and a few other soldiers, had been ill for days. Finally one morning, he informed us that we would take a day or two of rest and should not break camp. Munoz and the three other soldiers were isolated in a lean-to we had constructed and were cared for by Senor Pepito. At midday, after scanning the area for signs of

Cantos, Maximo left me gathering firewood a short distance from camp to relieve himself. He was no sooner out of sight when Cantos slid eerily from behind a large oak tree. He had a look of satisfaction on his bearded face. He addressed me in broken English to be assured I couldn't use a gap in communication to stall. "Senor Silas, a grand dead tree is fallen," he pointed over his shoulder in the opposite direction Maximo had gone and away from our camp. I hesitated desperate to save precious moments. A look of fury began to emerge on his face. He hissed his next words as he began to raise the rifle he held, "Come rapido…do you…refuse this order then?" There was a determined look in his eyes even as his lip still twitched out of apparent anger. Despite my feeling of defeat inside, I was determined to keep my head high. Obediently, I walked in the direction he ordered, away from safety. He allowed me to pass and then trailed me at a safe distance. He was a tall man, at least three inches taller than anyone else in the group. He was heavily muscled, not wiry muscle, like I had developed through years of hard living and modest eating. The respect given him by the other men came from intimidation due to his sheer strength. Power he demonstrated whenever an opportunity arose. After a short walk he spoke through clenched teeth. "Alto…err… stop," he commanded and slowly I turned to face him. He quickly tossed a large curved knife at my feet. The knife was not his. His knife was still attached to his belt. "Pick it up or I shoot you," he cautioned as a slight smile crept into the corner of his mouth. My mind was racing. Jumbled memories of my past began to drift around in my head like swirling snowflakes on a winter day. A clear understanding of self, filled the void. I was the boy who was constantly haunted by the inequality that existed in Roxbury. I was a boy who learned to be a man with a misunderstood people who others like me viewed as savages. I was now the man who learned what sweet Abigail patiently taught me years before about looking through other's eyes. Why had I stayed with my Spanish captors the last two years despite many opportunities to flee? These men had needed me. A sudden realization that Maximo would soon come frantically searching snapped me back to the present. It could cost my friend his life. I closed my eyes and lifted my head to heaven as I slowly began to bend my knees into a squat toward the knife on the ground. As my hand began to brush against the soft plants, I opened my eyes and looked directly into Cantos' devilish face. The sudden change in his expression, the confusion, convinced me he saw what I intended. He saw in me a look of understanding and acceptance. He recovered his anger after the brief moment and as I grasped the knife on the forest floor and began to rise, he took aim. He raised his rifle and centered his aim on my chest. I stepped forward and the shot rang out.

The shot took Cantos in the right side of his face and blood and brain fragments exploded from the left side of his head. His weapon fell to the ground harmlessly in front of his body, which collapsed to the forest floor slowly like a falling tree.

After a moment of shock, I glanced to the right to see Maximo just now lowering his rifle. He slowly looked to me with sadness in his eyes. The expression confused me for a moment. His words clarified the look. "There is no time my friend. Get his rifle and pouch and run. You are free."

Epilogue

I traveled day and night the first two days. Cautiously, I avoided any evidence of man while heading north. The experiences of the past seven years had taught me where I was supposed to go. Before reaching that final destination, there were stops that needed to be made. For more than two weeks, mountains to the east forced me to continue north. Daily ascent to high ground gave me a lay of the eastern landscape. Eventually, the Appalachian mountains (as I learned later the locals called them) slid away and I pushed on northward until finding the southern shores of the great lake Jean-Luc, Claude, and I had discovered years earlier. My path was now east where there were debts to pay. Eventually small settlements began to pop up. At first, the settlers had no knowledge of the town called Bickford. Soon I was directed northeast by some kindly folk who seemed familiar with the town.

After finding Bickford, locating Amos Perkins and his wife proved easy. The kind farmer and his kin still lived in the clearing they had years earlier. They didn't recognize me at first, being scruffier and fully-grown. As soon as I brought up the late night intrusion, they remembered the whole story in detail without being reminded. Amos was instantly apologetic for the beating the men had inflicted. I interrupted, "My purpose here is not to get an apology but to make amends for a debt I owe you. The kindness your family showed me despite the circumstances of our acquaintance taught me a great deal." He refused my request to repay him with a week's labor at first, but seeing my commitment or maybe recognizing my need to make amends, he agreed. At the end of a week we shook hands, shared in a drink, and parted ways. Upon departure, I headed due east in search of the farmer whose rifle and other materials I had stolen. My vague recollection of the landscape and event made the search a failure.

A few days later, after years of conflicted dreams about the moment, the town of Roxbury came into sight. Despite some fear of being arrested, I strode, head up, through the center of town and wordlessly headed toward my parents' house on the outskirts of town. Curious glances were cast my way as they are with any stranger, but there seemed to be no signs of recognition. The homecoming was far better than expected. My mother sprinted from the house and up the road, past my father who was working near the barn, as soon as I came into sight. She would tell us later she recognized my walk even from a great distance. Father followed slowly, curiously after her and didn't start moving with urgency until Mother and I embraced. To my surprise, Father joined in the happy reunion with tears in his eyes. We spent the rest of the late fall day feasting while both insisted on hearing every detail of the nearly seven years of adventure. It was very rewarding to see the amazement and admiration in both of their eyes. Though smiling, tears streamed down my mother's face when I showed them my scarred back and mutilated left hand that had gripped the sword blade while saving the Spanish surveyor, Gaspar Odalis. Two of my fingers still refused to work properly. Being there, safe in the moment, brought an appreciation of the fact that some greater power had made it possible to finally be home. My parents sent for my brother Micah, who now had a wife and his own piece of land nearby. He arrived with his wife and two young children. He embraced me without reservation and the tale was retold to the new listeners who sat in joyful anticipation of each new chapter. Micah would later make great sacrifices to encourage and help me write this story down.

Reverend Washburn had long since been re-assigned. My parents were not sure what would happen if my presence was discovered. There was surely some who still blamed me for the sickness years earlier. My parents prodded about a plan for the future, I assured them there was a plan but was intentionally vague. Father reminded me of how headstrong I had been, but marveled at how much the years had changed me. He joked about how determined Washburn was to save my troubled soul. "As if the man had never seen a spirited young man before," he snickered. "I knew you wouldn't stay put in that holding cell." The comment brought back the memory from years before of the piece of flint and sharp metal that had first inspired thoughts of escape. The gift I had always assumed mother was responsible for. "I knew you would know what to do," he smiled. It was embarrassing to remember the amount of times I had cursed this man over the last seven years. He was the one who had believed in me most.

At the end of the second day, just as my mind was spinning around the complexity of arranging a safe meeting with Abigail Reed, a lone figure strode up the road to my parents' cabin just before sunset. As Abigail came into view, my parents looked on with surprise, apparently still unaware of our secret friendship. "Miss Reed and I have some unfinished business to discuss," I said over my shoulder while creeping hesitantly down the steps and seeking a private conference with her.

The door to the cabin closed quietly behind me as I strode forward.

Many times over the last seven years I had dreamed of this moment. Never once had I imagined her coming to seek me out. The anticipated fear of the moment was missing, replaced by a feeling of relief. No matter how this meeting turned out, simply making it here was a great success. Many times in the last seven years, the perils surrounding me had brought doubt of this meeting ever taking place. As she came closer, finally the expression on her face was visible. Abigail was even more beautiful than memories had served and she wore a bright smile.

"Two days since you walked through town and no visit," she playfully scolded. "I was beginning to think my eyes had deceived me. Then I recalled that it had always been I who sought you out. Where did you go? Where have you been these long years?"

And so the long story was told again to Abigail as the sun set on a cool fall evening. She reacted just as the others had, amazed and full of questions. Upon conclusion of the story, staring into her eyes, I let my vulnerability show. "You were with me the whole time. Whenever danger approached, starvation loomed, death stalked, the thought of this moment kept me going, the thought of this moment gave me hope."

She cried. Tears of happiness, tears of joy ran down her face. She explained that her parents had tried to make her marry years before. Many suitors had come to call but she had stubbornly refused. Her father blamed it on the fierce independence she had shown since childhood, never suspecting that it was her commitment to a lost love. She had been waiting, believing deep in her heart that I was alive and would come back someday. With eyes full of curiosity, she asked what came next.

I told her about the land in the foothills, where the Frenchmen had taken me years before on the first trapping excursion to the mountains. The feelings and the dreams the hills had inspired in me. Her eyes filled with hope when she heard about the dream where she held our child. She insisted that we leave before sun-up the next morning. She refused to return home. She had snuck out of her parents' home after going to bed early with a fake illness. She was afraid they would force her to stay. My parents had reservations at first but soon admitted to uncertainty over what would transpire if the whole town knew of my return. Abigail had come with nothing, so mother sacrificed all that she could to start us on our way. We left before the sun rose the next morning. The excitement in Abigail's face relieved me of any doubt. It was as if she had waited for this moment her whole life. I knew exactly how that felt. We did not go directly to the foothills, as it was too late in the fall. We stayed the winter with the kind Amos and Mercy Perkins, who received us enthusiastically, before moving on in the spring. We lived out our days in that special place I had discovered with the French fur trappers Jean-Luc and Claude. We built our home, raised many children, and heard the music together.

Glossary of Words
with Historical Significance

meetinghouse: A house or building, often at the center of a village, for religious and/or political meetings.

stocks: A wooden structure used to confine individuals for punishment.

nightwalking: Wandering in a community or wooded areas at night; a crime in some colonial communities.

barn raising: A party usually providing food, drink, etc., for the purpose of assisting a neighbor to put up a new barn.

purgatory: Any condition or place of temporary punishment, suffering, or the like.

magistrate: A civil officer empowered to administer and enforce the law.

blasphemy: To speak of or address something sacred in a disrespectful manner.

flint rock: A hard quartz that sparks when struck with steel.

costrel: A leather or wooden container for holding water or other fluids.

condemned: To find guilty of a crime.

switch: A thin flexible rod, stick, twig, or whip.

breechcloth: A cloth worn about the buttocks and loins.

rendezvous: A meeting place or meeting arranged in advance.

peepers: A person's eyes.

mission: A religious settlement used to preach, teach, and convert Native American Indians to Christian faiths.

wigwam: A dwelling used by some North American Indians, typically consisting of an arched or cone-shaped framework covered with bark or hides.

garrison: A military installation, often a permanent one.

pulpit: An elevated platform with a lectern used in preaching or conducting a church service.

indenture: A contract obligating one party to work for another party usually in exchange for passage to the New World.

rapier: A longer, heavier sword, especially of the 16th and 17th centuries, having a double edged blade and used for slashing and thrusting.

ACKNOWLEDGMENTS

A special thanks to my wife Michele and Krista Reville for providing the support I needed to have the confidence to complete this project.

I would also like to thank Ronnie LaPlante, Avi Stark, Jim Claus, Katie Elsworth, and my parents, James and Nancy Renner, for their support and insightful contributions that helped shape the completed form of the story. And a special thank you to S.A. Wood for the back cover design. Despite not knowing whom the author was, several members of Krista Reville's 2013–2014 seventh grade English class at Schuylerville Central School also provided written feedback that contributed to the final version of this story. Thank you to Lindsey Fish, Paul Harshbarger, Mike Lanfear, and Rachael VanKeuren for their efforts.

Thank you to my editor, Darcy Scelsi, for her attention to detail and suggestions on improving the story.

ABOUT THE AUTHOR

D.J. Renner grew up in Stillwater, New York. He earned a Bachelor's degree in Business Management and a Master's Degree in Secondary Education from The College of Saint Rose in Albany, New York. He is a social studies teacher in upstate New York.

D.J. married his high school sweetheart Michele and they have three children. He spends his free time coaching, reading, writing, and attending his children's various athletic events. He loves to take vacations with his wife and family and always tries to take in a game at the nearest professional sports venue when traveling.

D.J. is currently working on his third book, *Little Land of Loose Ends*. Visit djrennerbooks.com for more information or to join D.J. Renner's mailing list for more details about upcoming projects.

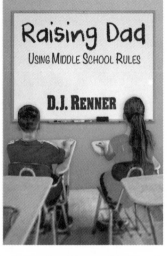